THE NINJA MICE OF WALL STREET

PREFACE

The ideas and characters in this book were conceived on June 20, 2014. On that fateful Friday morning, 8 year old Harrison and his dad, Tom, were heading cut for school. On the way out and in a rush, Harrison accidentally slammed the door on his fingers. The site of blood and pain of crushed little fingers were unbearable for both parent and child. His cries went unabated for nearly an hour. The original plans for their respective day went out the window. Instead of school or work, Harrison and his dad spent the whole day together. Their conversation somehow took them down path of imaginary mice characters. The idea for Ninja Mice was born. Little by little, the ideas and this book came together.

The characters and the stories herein this book are intended to entertain young readers with fun, funny and exciting adventure tales. Hopefully, it will also inspire them learn more about the geography, world events, history, facts and ideas introduced in this book. We think children will enjoy learning with humour and new vocabulary while parents will appreciate the wide range of ideas and topics covered by way of responsible and relatable themes. Hope you enjoy our book.

Tom & Harrison Szutu

The Ninja Mice of Wall Street – Return of the Rats
Published by Elusive Origin Books
Written by Tom Szutu and Harrison Szutu
Graphics by Tom Szutu
Ninja Mice illustrations by Ginette Palmer
Edited by Bruce Palmer
Copyright © 2016 by Tom Szutu

ISBN # 978-0-9918390-2-5

The moral rights of the authors have been asserted.

The writing process and how the book came together:

My son, Harrison, has always been a gifted reader. But his writing skills did not always match reading abilities. This book project began two years ago when Harrison was 8 years old as a way to encourage and motivate him to develop his writing skills. Little by little, the ideas and characters in this book came together. We had spent countless hours brainstorming and writing. Since then, I've taken all those ideas and pulled it together into a book. The project became much bigger than we ever imagined. Our goal for this book is not to make a fortune. It is for us to someday look back and say, "**Yeah, we did it. We published a book.**"

Available on Amazon.com and Lulu.com
Feedback is always welcomed. Visit us at facebook.com/NinjaMice

INTRODUCTION

A looooooooooong time ago, in a sewer system deep, deep, under New York City, lived four ninja mice. They lived in a section of the sewers known as New Mouse City. There the mice were taught the ancient ways of the Chi Energy Force by their teacher, Grandmaster Greenspan. They were known as the Ninja Mice of Wall Street, a beloved and courageous clan of mischievous do-gooders who believed in fairness and helping others.

The mice are enjoying a period of relative calm after defeating the evil Goldmouse Sachs and his rat army in their last epic battle. Since their victory, Grandmaster Greenspan has been away in his homeland of Japan. The mice were instructed by Greenspan to keep up their training and learn to harness their Chi Force powers. Life in New Mouse City and on Wall Street has returned to normal. But unbeknownst to the mice, Goldmouse is busy plotting his next move to take over the world with his mysterious new apprentice, Merrill Pynch.

CHAPTERS

Map of New York City

This Way to New Mouse City

Map of New Mouse City

(In the sewers under NYC)

5

Chapter One – A New Day

It was an early Monday morning in November. All was quiet in the Ninja Mice dojo in New Mouse City. Three of the mice were snuggled tightly in their comfy beds sleeping peacefully. One was not. All that could be heard throughout the dojo was the sound of little critters breathing. The one mouse not sleeping was Knyse (pronounced "n-eyes"). He was the leader of the Ninja Mice, a group of mischievous do-gooders who always helped others.

The peace and quiet in the dojo was abruptly broken by loud clanging sounds. **BANG BANG BANG BANG!!!** It was Knyse banging on an empty soup can with a wooden ladle. "**Come on guys, it's time to get up. Let's go, let's go!**" Knyse yelled.

The banging and yelling jolted Soros and Buffy out of bed. Their dizzy heads and blurry eyes were in a state of sleepy shock as they tried to get their bearings. But what about the third mouse, René? Well, he remained tucked under his blanket sound asleep with earplugs stuffed in his ears.

Annoyed by the sight of René still sound asleep, Knyse focused his Chi Force Energy. With a scrunched frowny face and a quick flick of his wrist, he yanked the blanket off of René. Then with a snap of his fingers and a wave of his hands, Knyse popped René's earplugs out and slapped his face with an ice cold wet towel. "**WHAAAAAA!** What a rude awakening," René screamed.

"Come on everybody, we've got to get up and get back to our training routine," Knyse yelled. "It's been three months since we've done any training and over six months since Grandmaster Greenspan left for Japan. He's going to be back very soon. Our lack of consistent training is making us lazy and weak."

"I know but I'm so tired and training is so hard. Can't we just have fun and play pranks instead." René complained.

"Knyse is right. Practice makes perfect. We must make hard what is soft. Make strong what is weak. We need to get back to our training," said Soros. "And I think we can do both. We can train to harness our new powers so that we can play better pranks!"

"Oh, that's a great thinking Soros," smiled René. "If I can learn to use my powers to drop Mentos into bottle of Diet Coke from far away, I won't get soaked next time."

"Ha, I warned you, René, not to play with my foods and cooking ingredients," said Buffy. "When you add Mentos to Diet Coke, it explodes! The mess you made in my kitchen was awful! Cooking is a lot like chemistry experiments. When you mix the wrong ingredients together, you could get a pretty nasty surprise in the kitchen or in your tummy if you eat it."

"Okay guys, let's go to the gym," Knyse shouted as he ushered everyone out of the bedroom. Down the hall they went and into the gym they called the Dungeon – a spacious room filled with an assortment of ninja weapons, exercise machines, and punching bags on one side. On the other side of the room was an obstacle course that resembled a supersized McDonalds Play Place with lots of added extra features like booby traps, water guns, water balloons, catapults, Nerf guns and fake doggie doo. Sometimes the doggie doo was real, all thanks to the resident prankster, René. So unlike the real McDonalds Play Place where removing your shoes before going on is mandatory, keeping your shoes on for the obstacle course is highly recommended. René would often say, "You've got to watch your step around here!" The goal of the obstacle course is to stay dry and complete it in less than 2 minutes as the other three mice operate the guns and catapults. So far, no one has been successful.

Mon	Tues	Wed	Thurs	Fri	Sat	Sun
Weapons & Kempo Striking punching and kicks	Plyometric jumping and leg exercises	Weight Training lift & push weights	Yoga	Grappling wrestling and jujitsu	Calisthenics suspension bands and pull up bars	Hamster Wheel Treadmill Run

"So guys, here is our weekly training schedule" Knyse said. "And because it's Monday, we are going to do striking and weapons training today!"

The mice all stood together in a ready-to-attack fighting stance. Their left hip, shoulder and lead leg pointing forward; feet are shoulder width apart; knees slightly bent and bouncy and fists up at chin level ready to strike or block. **Left-jab, right-cross, left-uppercut, right-elbow**. The mice called out and stepped forward with every punch and elbow strike thrown. Next they practiced Muay Thai knee strikes. The stance for this technique is similar to the previous fighting stance except instead of leading with one side of the body, you face your opponent with your chest square in front of them. The hands are also slightly opened and held high near eye level ready to protect your head from high kicks or grab your opponent's head. When attacking with knee strikes, you take a small step forward with your lead leg and plant that foot firmly as you grab your opponent by their head. Then thrust your other leg and knee upward at your opponent's head as you force their face down towards your upcoming knee. Power comes from driving your hips forward.

Becoming a true ninja is neither easy nor as quick as one might like. It requires many years of hard work and dedication. Even as one becomes a master or a grandmaster, a true ninja can never stop learning and improving. Although the mice have always been brave and chivalrous, they only started training to be ninjas and learning about the Chi Force after they met Grandmaster Greenspan. The mice were discovered by Greenspan when they were very young. At the time when they first met, Greenspan was in New York City on a business trip. Greenspan felt a strong Chi Force presence in the air that he could not ignore. He followed the Force down to the sewers underneath Wall Street and into New Mouse City. There Greenspan found the mice and immediately sensed their strong Chi Energy Force. The mice did not know of the Chi Force, what it was or what it meant to have it. All they knew was that once in a while, weird things would happen around them. But Greenspan did. He knew the mice had great potential so he took it upon himself to teach them the ways of Chi Force and how to harness and use its powers.

Grandmaster Greenspan

A wise and skilled **Asumari** grandmaster of the Chi Energy Force, Greenspan is one of the oldest and longest living mice in history. It is believed that he is at least 800 years old and practically a living history book. Once a strong and mighty mouse, Greenspan is nearing the end of his life in the physical world. His body is now frail and weak but he is strong with the Chi Force. Greenspan's connection with the Chi Force makes him very powerful and it gives him the energy to live a long life. His powers include the ability to sense impending attacks, read and influence the thoughts of others, levitate objects, channel his Chi Force to produce an energy blast and accelerate healing for himself and for others with his touch.

Knyse the Cheese Trader

He is the brains and strategic thinker of the Ninja Mice clan. As such, Knyse is often the voice of reason for the mice. He likes to take a calm and cautious approach in dangerous situations when others rush in impulsively. As one of Greenspan's best and most dedicated student, Knyse leads the Ninja Mice in fighting the evil forces that would take over the world. Although he is strong with the Chi Force, his skills and ability to use it are still at a beginner's level. Knyse got his name trading cheese with adult mice on the floor of the New York Stock Exchange when he was a kid. Trading was such a popular activity that eventually the adult mice traders established the Mouse International Cheese Exchange Market in New Mouse City. In terms of his personality, Knyse has a short hot tempered so don't pester him! And if you play a prank on or cross him, he will stew on ways to get even. He has a great sense of humour and likes to tell jokes. Puns are his favourites. Knyse also loves reading, playing chess and studying science, especially dinosaurs and animal documentaries. He often says he wants to be a paleontologist or a zoologist when he grows up. Physically, Knyse is small and skinny and likes to tell others that he is SSD... small, sweaty and deadly. That's because he does not like to take showers or bathe. His weapon is a red bladed Katana. The blade is red because it was infused with blood when the sword was made. When others say "nice" as in "nice work" or "nice job" or they mispronounce his name, he likes to correct them and say, **"Nnnnnno, it's not nice. It's n-eeeeyes."**

Soros the Sewer Rat

When Grandmaster Greenspan first met Soros in the sewers of New Mouse City, Greenspan thought Soros was a rat. That's

because Soros, who is in fact a mouse, towers over everyone else with his size and strength. He is one of the biggest and strongest mice that have ever lived. But his tough exterior is the complete opposite to who he is on the inside. Soros is actually one of the nicest, most gentle and kindest mice ever. Soros is quiet, loving and well-mannered as he always remembers to say please and thank you. He is so polite that many suspect that he is originally from Canada! Of all the Ninja Mice, he is the most mature. It's no wonder why all the girls like him. Soros is also very giving as he always shares with others. Of the three **gunas** present in all living beings, the guna of goodness and guna of passion are very strong in Soros. The guna of ignorance (or darkness) is very weak in him. When Soros sees others are hurt or suffering or bullied, Soros feels compelled to take action. His passion and restless energy does not allow him to be a passive observer of injustice. When he is not saving the world, Soros can be found practicing with his favourite weapon the Bo Staff or playing sports or playing his musical instruments. He loves all kinds of sports but his favourite is hockey. His favourite musical instruments to play are the piano and guitar. If Grandmaster Greenspan had a favourite student, it just might be Soros!

Rheneas the Rascal

His friends call him René (they shortened his name because he is short) is the smallest but best skilled fighter of the Ninja Mice. He is fearless, confident and a little reckless sometimes as he acts without thinking. René's speed and reflexes are lightning quick. His weapon of choice is a pair of Tonfas. René is also the light hearted fun loving joker of the group. He enjoys playing pranks on everyone and anyone. And just like Knyse, he also loves puns and other jokes too. When he is not training to be a ninja master or planning a prank, René is playing sports. He loves sports! Soccer and swimming are his favourite activities and he loves being outdoors. René is a highly active extravert with lots of high energy. He would rather be outside all the time doing anything than be inside studying. René is not someone who can sit still. His metabolism is also very high and as a result, he can eat anything and everything and never gain weight. As a young child, René was often bullied and picked on for his small size by the bigger kids. This motivated him to learn to defend himself and resulted in him becoming a skilled fighter. But before he learned self defense, René used humour to make friends with bullies so that they would stop picking on him.

Greenspan's first encounter with René was in a public washroom. The Chi Force Energy led Greenspan to a toilet stall where René was setting up a prank. Behind the closed door of the toilet stall, René was busy wrapping the toilet with clear plastic cling wrap. Doing so meant that anyone coming to use the toilet to relieve themselves would end up making a mess. If the person came in to do #1, they would end up spraying pee all over themselves. If the person needed to do #2, they would end up sitting on their own poop. From the other side of closed door, Greenspan sensed René's mischievous spirit. So instead of introducing himself right away, Greenspan played along and knocked on the door. "Excuse me I need to use the toilet," Greenspan said.

"It's all yours, sir," said René as he quickly dashed off around the corner ready to laugh and expecting to hear screams of anguish at any moment. As Greenspan entered the stall, he saw the trap. Fortunately though, he did not actually need to use the toilet. After waiting for a few minutes, Greenspan calmly and causally walked out like nothing happened. Watching from his hiding spot, René was mystified. Feeling confused, he walked up to Greenspan and asked, "Is everything all right, sir?"

"Of course," replied Greenspan softly as he looked into René's eyes to influence his thoughts. He suggested, "Nothing is wrong. But you have to use the toilet now. You do not see the plastic wrap. There is no plastic wrap covering the toilet." Without hesitating, René walked into the stall to pee and immediately ended up spraying and splashing all over himself. The shock of getting caught in his own prank made him realize that Greenspan was no ordinary stranger. From that moment on, René wanted to learn everything he could from him.

Buffett the Biscuit Thief

Nicknamed Buffy as he is a little overweight is everyone's best friend. This Nunchaku wielding mouse is both charming and friendly and fun to be around. Buffy's love of food is legendary. He loves to eat, eats all the time, likes to try new foods and is a great cook too. It is because of Buffy the Ninja Mice have a tradition they call Food Friday. Every Friday, they would try something new or something they haven't had in a long time. It doesn't matter what it is – it can be healthy, unhealthy, junk food, a drink or even a candy – so long as it is new or something they haven't had in a long time. And if they try the item and don't like it, they still have to finish the whole thing. So that means they can't go "oh yuck, this is gross, I'm not eating it" and throw it away. No, they have to eat all of it. Like his fellow ninja mice, Buffy's favourite foods include a love for sushi, pizza, pho and In-N-Out burgers. Because Knyse is an extremely slow eater, Buffy will often help him finish his meals. It's a mutually beneficial relationship. Buffy's snack cravings include gourmet European cheese, gelato, dark chocolate, pastries (especially macarons), bubble tea, cookies, and of course biscuits! When it comes to trying new candies, he likes to collect the wrappers as a memento. For meals, Buffy enjoys fine dining equally as much as comfort food at a greasy hole in the wall. He can get dressed up to dine with kings and queens or just eat leftover beans.

Buffy got his name when he was very young and living in an orphanage. At night he would sneak out of his room to steal snacks from the cupboard. In the morning, the adults running the orphanage would find a trail of biscuit crumbs from the cupboard back to Buffy's bed. This happened so often that the adults eventually put a padlock on the cupboard. But Buffy's insatiable craving for night time munchies drove him to learn how to pick locks and cover his tracks afterwards. His lock picking skills come in handy these days as he is an amateur escape artist and magician. His best magic trick is of course making food disappear. When Grandmaster Greenspan and Buffy first met, it was at the orphanage. Greenspan pretended to be a powerless fumbling old mouse. He played the part so well that he dropped the sandwich he was eating. It was on the ground for only a moment. Buffy immediately asked, "Hey mister, are you going to finish your sandwich?" Buffy is a big believer in the 2 second rule where if it's on the ground for less than 2 seconds, you can pick it up and eat it. Sometimes he'll stretch it to 5 seconds!

The Chi Energy Force

The Chi Force is an energy that exists in all living things. It flows, surrounds, penetrates and binds all living things together in the universe. More important y, this energy force connects all living thing together as one and it gives rise to consciousness. Those who are attuned and sens tive to the Chi Force can connect with it, channel its power and use the energy to do many things. The energy itself, like all other energies, follows the rule of energy conservation. That means it cannot be created or destroyed. The amount of Chi Energy and what is in the un verse now is what it will always be and what it has always been. The energy can only be transformed or transferred. Not all of the properties of the Chi Force are fully understood yet, not even by grandmasters like Greenspan. New aspects are being discovered all the time. It was recently discovered that certain planetary alignments in the solar system can alter or enhance the Chi Force and those who are attuned to it. This discovery explains why on nights when there is a full moon, those who are trained to use the power of the Chi Force were able to grow up to 1000 times their original size. For those who were merely Chi Force sensitive, weird things would often happen around them when a full moon appeared.

Asumari

An Asumari (a-soo-mar-i) is a ninja who has completed a certain level of training in the ways of the Chi Energy Force and has attained the rank of Master or higher.

For someone like Grandmaster Greenspan to recognize another Chi Force sensitive being is easy. For the rest of us newbies and aspiring ninjas, here is a handy little chart:

Strong Brave Ninja	Chi Force Sensitive Ninja
Courage comes from strong muscles	Courage comes from the heart and connection to other living beings
Cares about and empathic to others	Is one with others
Not afraid of anyone or anything	Looks for and sees the good in everyone and everything
Confident and pleased with own learning and skills	Is highly self-critical and often wanting things to be perfect
Is interested	Is highly curious
Is attentive	Is mentally and physically involved
Has good idecs	Has wild and silly ideas
Listens with interest	Shows strong feelings and opinions
Understands	Constructs abstractions
Grasp meanings	Draws inference
Completes projects	Initiates projects
Is receptive	Is intense
Copies accurctely; a technician	Creates new designs; an inventor
Good memorizer	Good guesser
Is alert	Is keenly observant
Knows the answer	Ask questions
Absorbs information and new ideas	Manipulates information and plays with new ideas
No weird or strange feelings	Lots of weird and strange feelings

Chapter #2 – Let's Do Yoga

The Ninja Mice have been working hard and training consistently every day since Monday. Their little bodies are sore and achy from all the hard work. It is now Thursday, yoga day; a day for stretching, meditating and deep thinking. Yoga is an ancient discipline used to focus the mind and spirit, strengthen the body and promote health and relaxation.

"**Namaste** my fellow Ninja Mice," Knyse shouted. "It's yoga time so let's all get into a relaxed state of mind, clear our heads and stretch out our sore mousey muscles."

All the mice, except Knyse, stumbled out of bed and into the dungeon. It's 7 in the morning and they're tired and groggy. But unlike the beginning of the week, Knyse did not have to bang on a soup can or throw a cold wet towel on anyone's face to wake them up. The mice are getting back into their routine and getting used to waking up early again. "It's a great day for Yoga," Knyse continued. "When you find peace within yourself, you become the kind of mouse who can live at peace with others."

"Isn't yoga supposed to be relaxing?" René asked sarcastically. "Because I was very relaxed and at peace 5 minutes ago back in my bed. Can I please go back there to be at peace? Huh, can I?"

"That's a good one, little buddy" said Soros to René as he grinned proudly at his own wit. Buffy laughed along too. But Knyse was not pleased by René's back talking and grumbled at Soros and Buffy for not siding with him. Knyse felt Soros and Buffy's lack of support only served to encourage disrespect and laziness. He fumed at the others as an awkward silence filled the room. But deep down inside, Knyse thought the joke was funny too as he also wanted to go back to his comfy bed and curl up in his pillows. It's no fun for him to be on all the time and have to be the one to keep everyone on task. Knyse wanted to have a day off too. So the more he thought about the joke, the more he began to crack. Everyone saw Knyse's smile beginning to show until he couldn't hold it in anymore. The silence was finally broken by everyone's spontaneous and uncontrollable laughter.

"Ok, that was a good one René. But let's get to doing yoga so we can have breakfast afterwards. I'm starving already," Knyse said cheerfully.

The mice began to do their yoga poses. The dungeon was still and quiet for the most part with Knyse calmly calling out the different poses from time to time. **Asanas** (manner of sitting) is any yoga posture or pose while **Vinyasa** is any flowing sequence of poses linked together. "Sun Salutation…" Knyse called out. "Now repeat Warrior I to Warrior II" Knyse added. Then "Cobra… Upward Dog… Downward Dog… and repeat."

An hour into yoga, the mice continued to do their poses. As they stretched their little bodies, everyone's attention started to turn to food. Soros and Buffy being the two bigger mice were especially hungry and impatient. René inquired about breakfast. "Hey, what's for breakfast today? Can we have our Halloween candies? I've got a craving for a Kit Kat and some Smarties."

"No can do, René," replied Knyse. "We have to save our candies to go shopping later today. We'll need them for trading at the Flea Market. We especially have to save the coffee crisps chocolate bars. They're the most valuable because everybody *looooves* coffee crisp!"

"Don't worry, I'll make you guys something special for breakfast." Buffy reassured René.

Downward Dog: Performed by making an upside down letter "V" with your body and with your hands and feet on the ground while your bum pointed up in the air. The hands shoulder-width apart, placed firmly on the ground. Feet are hip distance apart, weight evenly distributed between hands and feet, with heels pushing toward the floor.

While in the Upward Dog position, the mice were breathing deeply and all was calm and quiet. Everyone's attention was turned inwards as it should be. They could feel the Chi Force Energy in the universe flowing around and through them. But suddenly, a loud "**GRRRRRRR**" was heard. It was the sound of hungry pain of an empty stomach. "Quiet" muttered Knyse as he tried to maintain inner focus. But the "**GRRRRRRRRR**" returned moments later and louder. "QUIET" muttered Knyse more forcefully matching the growl's rise in volume. This time, room remained silent a bit longer as though the hunger was scared away by Knyse's rising temper. But that was not to be the case as the loudest "**GRRRRRRRRRRRRR**" yet heard returned. "**I SAID QUIET**" Knyse yelled at the top of his lungs losing all inner focus. But the silence did return to the room. And this time it remained. Knyse tried to reclaim his inner peace as he called out the next pose. "Downward Dog," he squeaked. As everyone got into their pose with their derrière pointed up to the ceiling, an unmistakably loud and smelly fart "**BRRRRRRRRRR**" ripped out.

"**OH MY GOD! Yoga over! Yoga over!**" Knyse yelled as everyone cleared the room in a hurry. The culprit and innocent victims alike all ran from the scene of the crime. The mice all regrouped in the kitchen. Everyone was still holding their noses while their mouths were hanging wide open. They were out of breath and gasping for fresh air. "Dude, who cut the cheese?! I want a confession right now," Knyse demanded.

"Not me," said Soros.

"Whoever smelled it, dealt it," René teased.

"My farts don't stink," Buffy joked.

"Oh brother" said Knyse as he rolled his eyes at Buffy. "Your gas emissions do stink. They're silent, but violent!" he mocked.

"Ha ha, nice one," laughed Soros. Upon hearing this, Knyse and René looked at each other and together said, "**Nnnnnno, it's not nice.**" They paused for a moment and Soros joined in with them and said, "**it's n-eeeeyes**" and immediately erupted into laughter.

Buffy also laughed. He has a good sense of humour and can take a joke. Buffy then went about to make breakfast for the group while everyone else set the table and waited with great anticipation. Not only does Buffy consider himself a foodie, but he loves to cook as well. It is one of his favourite ways to show love. Some folks show love with words while others do it with gifts or hugs and kisses. Buffy shows it with food. He cares for, nourishes and feeds his friends with lots of delicious foods. This is especially true around the holiday season and during times of celebrations. During these times, Buffy will often put on a big fancy production. It's a lot of hard work for him but it makes him feel good to see everyone enjoying the fruits of his labour.

It didn't take long for Buffy to finish making breakfast. On the menu for everyone today was:

~ *3 Pancakes topped with sweet Canadian maple syrup*
~ *3 lean sausages and 2 eggs sunny side up*
~ *½ cup of fresh wild blueberries with avocado slices*
~ *Glass of freshly squeezed orange juice*

"Wow, this looks so good," said one of the mice. "Smells good too," said another. "Taste even better," said Soros as he chowed down.

Breakfast is the most important meal of the day and every meal should have a good amount of all 3 types of nutrients (called macro-nutrients) – carbohydrates (carbs), protein and fats. All the foods we eat can be divided into different groups such as meats, dairy or fruits and vegetables. But no matter what groups they belong to, they all have some combination of the 3 types of nutrients.

The maple syrup, orange juice and blueberries are a good source of instant sugar your body can use immediately for fuel. And like all fruits, the orange juice and blueberries are a good source of vitamins that your body needs. The pancakes, sausages, eggs and avocado slices are a healthy source of carb, protein and fats. This part of the meal will take longer for your body to breakdown and convert to a usable source of energy called glucose. As your body slowly breaks down your breakfast, your body will have the energy it needs to fuel itself until your next meal or snack. If at breakfast, you took in more calories than your body needs before the next meal, you'll have too much glucose floating around in your bloodstream. Your body will then turn the excess into glycogen and store it away for you to use later when you don't eat enough. This is body fat.

On average, a young and active growing body needs somewhere between 1500 to 2000 calories a day. A big guy like Soros or an active little guy like René needs about 2200 calories a day. An average active kid like Knyse needs about 1800 while someone chubby like Buffy will need less than 1500 calories. The meal the mice had for breakfast was 500 calories.

It didn't take long for all but one of the mice to finish breakfast. The laggard was Knyse. He was slow as usual with half a pancake and a sausage left to go. Everyone urged Knyse to hurry up as they were eager to go to the Flea Market. "Dude, you're taking forever," they told him. Buffy offers to help Knyse finish. "Dude, let me help you with it," he said. But before he could say anything, Knyse felt an urge from his lower tummy region.

"Sure, go ahead and finish it for me. Thanks," Knyse said. "While you do that, **I'm going to go drop the kids off at the pool.**"

Soros, "you mean you have to go poo?!!"
Knyse, "yes, I have to go do a BM."
Soros, "a BM?"
Knyse, "yes, a bowel movement."

Everyone rolls their eyes because Knyse likes using euphemism for going to the toilet instead of actually saying he's going to use the toilet. Then it dawned on everyone that it's going to be awhile so they better go use the bathroom first before Knyse gets in there. Knyse is notorious for his lengthy visits to the toilet. He likes to sit and read. He can literally sit on the porcelain throne for hours to read to the frustration of everyone else who needs to use the bathroom. The other mice each rush to take their turn to go pee. An interesting fact about the mice is that at home they all like to sit down to pee. This is because sitting down to pee actually prevents splashing and mishaps like peeing on the seat or missing the bowl completely. They also don't flush the toilet immediately after use if they know someone else needs to use it right after them. Not flushing right away saves water and is more environmentally friendly. While the others rush to use the bathroom, Knyse is busy gathering a stack of his favourite books and comics for his reading pleasure.

Nearly an hour has gone by since Knyse barricaded himself in the bathroom. Not a sound, a peep or a squeak has been heard from him from the other side of the door. No moan or grunt either. The other mice can only be assumed their fearless leader is still sitting on his throne reading. But is it possible that he has fallen asleep? If so, it won't be the first time. They decide to knock on the door and check on him.

THUMP! THUMP! THUMP! "Hey Knyse, you done yet? Hurry up, dude. We gotta go!" they yelled.

Knyse replied, "Okay, give me a second." And right away he wrapped up what he was doing; washed his hands in the sink with soap and water; and picked up the pile of books that were stacked up next to the toilet. He then pressed the lever to flush the toilet. But instead of a gush of water and a familiar sound of contents going down the drain smoothly, Knyse heard a choking sound followed by a "**Clug, Clug, Clug...**" The toilet clogged!

"**UGGGH!**" Knyse screamed and cringed as he watched the toilet flow backup. The murky water level slowly rose. Little by little, it crept higher and higher until it reached the lip of the toilet bowl. At this point, Knyse was in full panic mode. The sewage water was still creeping higher and he knew it would overflow at any moment. The thought of it overflowing on to the floor and having to clean it up was absolutely sickening.

Knyse realized he had quickly gathered his sense and regain his composure. He had to act quickly and he knew he could not use his Chi Force powers when his mind is in chaos and panic. The Chi Energy can only flow through him when there is order and calm. Knyse focused himself. With his hands wide open, he used the Chi Force to hold back the sewage water from overflowing. He then pushed the blockage down with a quick thrust of his open hands. The blockage moved only slightly, but it was just enough to stop the threat of an overflow. Knyse is strong with the Force, but his skills and ability to use his powers is still very weak. He is not yet strong enough to unclog the toilet by himself. He will need the help of the other mice. Knyse opens the bathroom door to call the others. "Hey guys. You'll never guess what happened... the toilet clogged and I can't unclog it on my own. Can you guys come in here and help me? With our combined powers we'd be strong enough to move the blockage." But the others refused to go into the bathroom to help him.

"Oh no way! I'm not touching **THAT** with my powers. That's gross," said René.

"Would love to help you, but the stench... it's just too much for me. Sorry. **EEEW**," said Soros.

"I love my delicious breakfast," said Buffy. "If I go in there, I'm going to lose my breakfast... I don't want to lose it. Sorry, Can't help you. And besides, we want to get going to the market."

"Oh great, now we're going to have to pick up a plunger from the market too," Knyse complained. But he knew he was not going to win this argument. Reluctantly, he accepted his fate and knew he would have to unclog the toilet the old fashioned way.

Chapter Three – Shopping at the Market

The mice gathered their things and headed out the door. They made their way across town from their dojo to the Flea Market through a series of tunnels and roadways. The market is a hub of activity and a busy place. Even on weekdays, it's usually crowded and noisy. And no matter what you're looking for, you'll likely find it there. Arriving at the Flea Market, the mice walk through a grand entrance way and see many friends and familiar faces. The most prominent figure they see is their old friend the Market Crier, Yellen. She is standing in the middle of the market on an elevated pedestal platform. She watches the market like a hawk.

Similar to a town crier, a market crier is an officer of the market who makes public announcements. They carry a hand bell which they ring to attract everyone's attention, as they shout the words *"Oyez, Oyez, Oyez!"* before making their announcements. The word "*Oyez*" means "*hear ye,*" which is a call for silence and attention. Oyez derives from the Anglo-Norman word for listen. In addition, criers are often dressed elaborately, by a tradition dating to the 18th century, in a red and gold coat, white breeches, black boots and a tricorne hat.

Yellen's job as the Market Crier is to decide which merchants are allowed into the Flea Market to trade. She also has to announce the daily opening and closing of the market and the specials of the day. But her most important role is to announce the market's interest rate and trading rates. The interest rate is the number of coffee crisp chocolate bars she will charge you to borrow something from her. For example, she will charge you 1 coffee crisp bar per day every day to borrow her shovel. The bars she charges you will not be returned to you when you return her shovel... nope, she eats them instead.

The trading rate is the number of coffee crisp chocolate bars she will give you or take from you in exchange for something you want. For example, if you want a shovel, she will give it to you in exchange for 5 coffee crisp bars. If you want to give her a shovel, she will give you 4 coffee crisp bars for it.

Yellen's rates are always the lowest rates available anywhere and from anyone. But not everyone or anyone can trade and borrow from her. She only deals with the biggest and safest merchants in the market. When borrowing, that means she will not lend you 1 shovel for 1 chocolate bar. Instead, she will lend you a minimum of 100 shovels for 100 bars per day, every day. Normally, she is likely to lend 1000 shovels at a time. Similarly when trading, she will not trade 1 shovel for 4 or 5 chocolate bars at a time. No, she would usually only trade 1000 shovels at a time for 4000 or 5000 chocolate bars... holy cow, think about the cavities you would get from eating all those chocolate bars! Your dentist would be happy! Yellen's rates typically do not affect any individual mice personally. But they do set the standard by which the merchants at the market will lend and trade with individual shoppers.

The Ninja Mice make their way over to center of the market to greet their old friend, Yellen. "Hey Yellen, how are you? How's your day?" They inquire. They also tell her they brought with them their Halloween candies to trade with and that they have quite a bit of coffee crisp chocolate bars. At the base of Yellen's pedestal is a board which list the merchant rates today for commonly traded items. On the board, it had the following rates:

1 Box of 10 Crayons = 1 Box of 50 Legos
1 Box of 10 Crayons = 5 coffee crisp
1 Box of 50 Legos = 5 coffee crisp
1 Bag of 1000 raisins = 5 coffee crisp
1 Block of cheese = 25 coffee crisp
1 Block of cheese = 5 Bags of raisins

Based on the posted merchant rates on Yellen's board, the mice were able to calculate the following exchange rates on their own:

10 Legos = 1 coffee crisp
2 crayons = 1 coffee crisp
200 raisins = 1 coffee crisp
5 Legos = 1 crayon
100 raisins = 1 crayon

20 raisins = 1 Lego brick
1 Block of cheese = 25 coffee crisps
1 Block of cheese = 5000 raisins
1 Block of cheese = 250 Legos
1 Block of cheese = 50 crayons

The mice came to the market with 30 coffee crisp chocolate bars. They were hoping to pick up some cheese, raisins, crayons and Legos. Knyse did not see what he was looking for on the board.

He asks, "By the way, Yellen, what's your rate today for a toilet plunger?" Before answering, Yellen begins to ring her bell and clear her throat...

Ding-Ding, Ding-Ding, Ding-Ding...
Hear Ye, Hear Ye, Hear Ye!
The rate for a toilet plunger today is 50 coffee crisp bars!
Ding-Ding, Ding-Ding, Ding-Ding...
Hear Ye, Hear Ye, Hear Ye!
The rate for a toilet plunger today is 50 coffee crisp bars!

Yellen always yells and repeats herself twice when making an announcement. Knyse tucking his head down and cringing with embarrassment as Yellen attracted much attention from other shoppers and merchants alike with her rate announcement. **"Cheeses!** Why so expensive?" Knyse asked.

"Well, if you need a toilet plunger, it's likely you are desperate." Yellen reasoned. "That means you're in no position to negotiate so don't argue with me about the rate! And I don't lend out plungers in case you were wondering. That's kind of gross." The mice realized Yellen's logic was correct. And that she was right about it being gross. They also knew that they could not afford something so expensive. "You guys might want to check with Mr. Mendeleev at the back of the market. He's a chemist and he may have an alternative solution for your problem," Yellen suggested. The mice thanked her and went on their way.

Yellen is a helpful and honest market official. She is not there to take advantage of or cheat anyone. She is simply there to make sure the Flea Market runs smoothly and to help promote trading so her job at the market is a very important one. And as the Flea Market Crier, Yellen is also the head of the Flea's Open Market Committee (FOMC). The **FOMC** is a group of Flea Market officials that meets every day before market open and after the market close to review trading activities of the day and evaluate their own rates to see if they need to change it or keep it the same.

As the Ninja Mice made their way through the market looking for the items they came for, they heard the sound of loud banging and clanging and chanting coming from the other side.

We Got Pots, We Got Pots
We Got Lots and Lots of Pots
We Got Pans, We Got Pans
We Got Lots and Lots of Pans

It was a couple of mice named Dilma and Lula banging on pots and pans to attract the attention of shoppers. It was annoyingly loud, but it certainly worked as it got Buffy's attention. "Hey guys," he said. "I know we didn't come here for pots or pans, but let's go check it out. We might find something really good for the kitchen." The other mice went along with the idea and they all followed the sound of the chants.

We got pots, we got pots
We got lots and lots of pots
We got pans, we got pans
We got lots and lots of pans

As the Ninja Mice walked up to the shop, Dilma greeted them, "Welcome to **Pedrobros**. I'm Dilma. Not only am I the President, I'm the first female President in this company's history. This is my business partner, Lula. What can we get for you today?"

"Well, I'm looking for some new cookware for my kitchen," Buffy replied.

Seizing the opportunity, Dilma jumped right in and said "Then you've come to the right place, because..." Dilma and Lula began to clang and chant again:

We got pots, we got pots
We got lots and lots of pots
We got pans, we got pans
We got lots and lots of pans

Lula brings several pots and pans to show Buffy. But every one of them seemed old, dirty or used. "They have dirty spots on them," Buffy quipped.

Dilma and Lula looked at each other and thought, "wow, that's fantastic!" and began to chant and clang:

We got spots, we got spots
We got lots and lots of dirty spots

"And they're cracked," Buffy added.

We got cracks, we got cracks
We got lots and lots of dirty cracks

"And they're rusty, too!"

We got rust, we got rust
We got lots and lots of dirty rust

Buffy was not impressed or amused by their antics. "What don't you have?" He asked mockingly.

"We have everything!" Dilma replied proudly.

"Oh, really? You have everything?" René chimed in. "Do you have underpants?" He asked sarcastically as he laughed to himself. Dumbstruck by René's inquiry, Dilma and Lula looked at each other confused. Turning their attention back to René, Lula offers to go to the back of the shop to look. Racing to the back, Lula quickly pulled down his pants and took off his underwear. He then ran back to the front and presented his underwear to René.

"**WHAT THE HECK!**" René screamed in horror and disgust. The underwear was obviously used as it was not wrapped in a package and was still warm to the touch. Not only that, it also had a stinky odor. René looked over to his friends and together they spontaneously erupted into a chant:

They got pants, they got pants,
They got lots and lots of dirty underpants

Buffy, René and the other Ninja Mice shook their collective heads and walked away from Pedrobros very unimpressed. They went back to look for the original items they came for – cheese, raisin, Legos and crayons. Based on their previous experience dealing with the merchants at the Flea Market, the Ninja Mice knew the following:

> **Mr. Monet** is a famous French artist. His paintings and drawings are very beautiful and valuable. He will usually only trade them for something equally very valuable. But Mr. Monet also has lots of crayons and wants to only trade them for raisins. He loves raisins.
>
> **Mr. Mus Christiansen** is a Lego collector and has lots of them. He wants only to trade them for crayons or cheese.
>
> **Mousel Fournier**, originally from France, is a food merchant. He is very successful because he will trade just about any

food items you might have or want. But one thing he will not do is split up his packaged items like raisins and cheese. He will not split his bag of 1000 raisins into smaller quantities. And he will most certainly not cut the cheese!!!

The Ninja Mice decided to visit with Mr. Fournier at his store to get their food items first. They had with them 30 coffee crisp bars which they traded with Mr. Fournier for a block of cheese (for 25 bars) and a bag of raisins (for 5 bars). Next they went over to Mr. Monet where the mice traded 500 of their raisins (half a bag) for 5 of his crayons. Lastly, they then went over to Mr. Christiansen to trade for his Legos. The mice could trade some of their crayons with Mr. Christiansen or cut a portion of their cheese for his Legos. They decided that it would easier to g ve him 2 crayons for 10 of his Legos than to cut the cheese. After all of their trades, the mice had the following items:

- 0 Coffee Crisp chocolate bars
- 1 Block of Cheese
- 500 Raisins (half a bag)
- 3 Crayons (less than a full box)
- 10 Legos (less than a full box)

The mice got everything they came for except a toilet plunger which was too expensive. Following on Yellen's suggestion, they went to speak with Mr. Mendeleev the chem st at the back of the market. Mr. Mendeleev is a kooky scientist with long frizzy hair and a full beard from Saint Mouseburg, Russia. He is always tinkering with elements and studying their properties. The mice found Mr. Mendeleev at his shop and told him about their little plumbing problem. Right away, Mr. Mendeleev had a solution for them. "My dear ninja friends," he said, "What you need is some sodium."

"Oh, we had a little bit at breakfast this morning," Buffy replied.

"No, no, no. I don't mean for you. I mean for your toilet. You need sodium for your toilet!" Mendeleev clarified.

"You want us to put salt into our toilet?!" the mice all asked in confusion.

"No, no, no. I don't mean sodium as in salt. I mean sodium as in the metal. You need pure sodium metal," Mendeleev explained. He went on to describe for the mice how sodium metal reacts with water by giving up one of its electrons. He noted that a

1 H		
3 Li	4 Be	
11 Na	12 Mg	
19 K	20 Ca	21 Sc
37 Rb	38 Sr	39 Y
55 Cs	56 Ba	57
87 Fr	88 Ra	89

small chunk of sodium will produce a small explosion when placed in water. Mendeleev then pulled out a table that he developed to explain how sodium (symbol Na) is an alkali metal that belonged to the Group 1 column. All the alkali metals in the Group 1 column had very similar properties. The big difference, however, is that the further down the column you go, the more explosive the metal is when placed in water. Starting at the top of the Group 1 column, lithium (Li) is the least reactive. But cesium (Cs) and francium (Fr) are the most reactive and are very unstable. In fact, francium is actually **radioactive**! Even a little bit of it can cause quite a big explosion. Because of their properties, cesium and francium are kept in very special containers.

This last bit of information caught René's attention. "Could we trade you some raisins for a sample of every alkali metal you have?" René asked.

"Oh yes of course. I love raisins," Mendeleev answered. "My rate is 100 raisins for 100 grams of metal."

All the mice love raisins too so they were reluctant to give any of it up. But they were equally as intrigued by the alkali metals as René was. The mice all agreed to do a trade with Mendeleev and they let René speak on their behalf. "Okay, we have 500 raisins so we'll take 100 grams of each alkali metal starting with sodium, to potassium, to rubidium, to cesium and francium."

But before agreeing to the trade, Mendeleev wanted to taste the raisins first. He wanted to make sure the quality was good and that it wasn't a bag of boogers or something like that. After sampling a few raisins to his satisfaction, Mendeleev and the mice completed their exchange. Afterwards, the mice were eager to get on with their day so that they could go home to try the sodium on their toilet.

Chapter Three
Bonus Skill Testing Questions

Dear Aspiring Ninjas

Can you solve the following exchange rate questions? If the Ninja Mice had 40 coffee crisp bars what items could the get by trading? Assuming a block of cheese cannot be cut...

- Could they get everything they came for?
- How many of each item could the get by trading?
- Can they get a block of cheese, a full box of crayons, a full box of Legos, a full bag of raisins and 100 grams of each alkali metals?
- How many combinations of items could the get?

Good luck little ninjas!

Periodic Table of the Elements

© 2014 Todd Helmenstine
science.notes.org

Lanthanide Series

Actinide Series

Alkali Metal · Alkaline Earth · Transition Metal · Basic Metal · Semimetal · Nonmetal · Halogen · Noble Gas · Lanthanide · Actinide

Chapter Four – Jeremy the Jerk

After shopping at the Flea Market yesterday, Knyse, Buffy and René went to the cinema and stayed out late partying – drinking Gatorade and bubble tea and eating dark chocolate and Sun Chips. Meanwhile, Soros went to visit Diana and her roommate Nadia. The other mice suspected Soros had a date with Diana or Nadia but he has not admitted to liking one of them – but ditching your buddies for a date with a girl… **not cool!** The trio would later learn the girls took Soros shopping at a mall – **totally not cool!** By the time they all met back at the Dojo last night, it was too late to deal with the toilet. In the morning, the mice did their grappling training and had breakfast afterwards. Now it was time to deal with the dirty work.

As was the case yesterday, Buffy, René and Soros refused to go into the bathroom. Knyse wasn't crazy about going in either. The smell did not get any better overnight. Standing just outside the bathroom door and holding their noses was plenty close for all of them. "Okay guys, here's the plan," Knyse said. "We'll wrap the chunk of sodium in toilet paper so that when it goes into the toilet, it won't react with the water right away. We should have a few seconds before the water soaks through the paper. I'll run into the bathroom to throw the wrapped sodium into the toilet. Then I'll use my powers to push the metal down to the bottom where the blockage is. Then I'll close the toilet lid cover. As soon as you hear me slam the lid down, you guys hold your breath and quickly run in and help me hold down the toilet lid. With our combined powers, we should be strong enough to hold down the lid. Any questions?"

"Why don't we try the francium?" René asked inquisitively as he was eager to try the highly volatile metal.

"Are you nuts?!" Knyse asked rhetorically. "Let's not overdo it. Based on what Mr. Mendeleev told us yesterday, the francium could blow up our entire bathroom. If the sodium doesn't work, we can try the potassium next."

Buffy and Soros agreed with Knyse's more cautious approach and proceeded as planned. "Okay, here we go. On three," Knyse said as he began to count, "1 – 2 – 3."

RUSH RUSH RUSH
THROW
SLAM
RUSH RUSH RUSH
3-2-1

ARRRGGG!!!

The toilet blew up splattering fecal matter everywhere and sewage rained down on everyone. The walls were covered as were the mice. The blockage cleared but the chunk of sodium proved too much. The mice all stood there in stunned silence.

"Okay... So... That was not part of the plan," said Knyse stating the obvious. "Glad we didn't use francium, huh?" he added.

"No kidding!!!" René retorted. "That was an **EPIC FAIL!!!**"

Soros knew at this point Knyse was feeling pretty bad about the situation. He knew he could join in with René to pile on and give Knyse a hard time or he could be kind. He could be the kind of friend that picks others up when they are down.

"I don't see that way, little buddy," said Soros to René. "I see this as a very successful learning experience. We have succeeded in learning what doesn't work. We learned a lot about the reactive property of sodium first hand and now we know we didn't have to use the entire chunk. From this experience, we can imagine the properties of the other alkali metals. All and all, I think it's been a very successful experiment."

Hearing Soros' kind words made Knyse feel better about himself. Soros' kind heart and never ending optimism is what makes him such a good friend and valuable member of the Ninja Mice clan. He never loses his temper and he always has something nice to say. No matter how bad the situation may be, Soros can always find the positive.

Buffy echoed Soros' sentiment and said, "That's a good way of looking at it. Failure is not always a failure, especially if when we learn from it. Failure is actually a better teacher than success. We only truly fail when we don't learn from our experiences."

Hearing Buffy echo Soros' positive message made Knyse forget about the disgustingness of the situation. Meanwhile, René reluctantly agreed with Buffy and Soros' point of view. A moment ago, René was fuming mad. But he realized that being upset wasn't going to change the fact that he was covered in poop. René realized he can be mad or he can have fun with the situation. "How often am I going to have the opportunity to throw poop at Knyse and get away with it?" he thought to himself. Seizing the moment, René wiped some of the mess off his face and flung it at Knyse, hitting him right in the forehead. Knyse could only smile at the ridiculousness of the situation as the other three laughed hysterically. It's hard to imagine how anyone can feel good standing in a room covered in poopy sewage with an exploded toilet, but that's what happens when you have good friends who care and will be there for you when you need them.

Any one of the mice could have walked out on Knyse leaving him alone to deal with the mess he created. But that's not what good friends do. "Let's all pitch in and help Knyse clean up so we can all go to Central Park and enjoy our Friday afternoon in New York City." Soros said. "And don't forget we're meeting with Jeremy for dinner tonight!"

"Oh yes, I can't wait till tonight," Buffy added. "It's a food Friday at Jeremy's and it's a full moon tonight, too!"

"What's the big deal about a full moon tonight? You're going to see one in a moment when I go take a shower," René joked.

The Full Moon Came Early Today!

René

With all the mice friends working together, it didn't take long for them to clean up. When they finished, the mice ventured into a tunnel that connected their dojo in New Mouse City to the streets of New York. As they surfaced, the mice are greeted by mild autumn weather and a gentle breeze. They are surrounded by towering skyscrapers and grand architectural designs. In front of them on the corner of **Wall Street** and **Board Street** was the historic New York Stock Exchange building – home of one of the oldest and biggest stock markets in the world.

Most people know Wall Street as the epicenter of global financial markets, capitalism and commerce. The location and name itself has become synonymous with making money, wealth and greed. As with many of the famous streets and roads in the world, Wall Street's origins have historical significance. Its name is a direct reference to a wall that was erected by Dutch settlers on the southern tip of Manhattan Island in the 17th century. During this time, a war between the English and Dutch threatened to spill over onto the island's American colonies. So the Dutch, located at the southernmost part of the island, decided to erect a defensive wall. The area was then referred to as Waal Straat in Dutch.

From where the mice surfaced, they walked over to the Wall St subway station to take the Line 4 (Green) metro train up to 59 St Lexington Ave station. Seeing mice on a train is not a big deal. Local New Yorkers and tourist alike are used to seeing them on the train so no one ever makes a fuss. Exiting on Lexington Avenue, the mice walk over to Central Park. The park is an urban paradise of greenery in what would otherwise be a concrete jungle in Manhattan – which is one of the five boroughs that make up New York City.

A short walk into Central Park, the mice come across Wollman Rink. Though the weather is still mild, skating season has begun. Many parents and children are out skating as are young couples in love. With Central Park as a romantic backdrop on one side and the majestic New York skyline on the other, Wollman Rink is an iconic skating rink. Everything about it is truly spectacular this time of year. The popular rink continues a legacy that began in the 19th century when skaters first flocked to the area's small lakes and ponds.

The mice spent the afternoon running and playing in Central Park as any carefree youngster should. They played hide-and-seek, tag, soccer, climbed trees and even a little 2-on-2 hockey. In the late afternoon, the mice took a walk into a more wooded area of Central Park. There they saw chipmunks and squirrels alike busy gathering food and preparing for winter. A voice from above in a tree calls out to the mice. "**Hello!**" The mice look up to see it was an owl. It was no one they knew but they reply back with a friendly hello of their own. "Aren't you guys the Ninja Mice from New Mouse City," the owl asked.

"Why, yes we are!" Knyse confirmed proudly.

Owl quickly flew down to greet the mice. Spreading his wings, he embraced the mice warmly. "It's an honour to meet all of you! Ever since you saved the city and everyone it, I've wanted to meet you. My name is **Murrow**. I watch everything that goes on here in Central Park. Nothing happens here without me knowing about it."

The Mice were touched by owl's gratitude. Murrow was referring to the event that took place more than a year ago when the Ninja Mice defeated the evil Goldmouse Sachs and his rat army. "What happened to Goldmouse after the battle?" Murrow asked.

"We don't know what exactly happened to him," Knyse replied. "We're not sure if he survived or died in the collapse during our big epic battle. We haven't seen or heard from him since so we think he must have perished."

"Let's hope so," said Murrow. "I also haven't seen or heard from him either. What about his Lieutenant, **Darryl Lynch**?"

"He died for sure," said Soros. "We saw it with our own eyes and felt his Chi Force Energy depart from his body. It's too bad because he actually wasn't so bad. We tried to save him, but he refused our help and chose to die instead."

"Well, that may be for the best," Murrow thought. He then warned the mice of a new potential threat. "I believe his name is Merrill Pynch. I've heard a lot about him but have only caught a quick glimpse once. He is very big and menacing looking. I've heard crazy stories that make me believe he is strong with the

Chi Force and a very powerful Asumari. Because I have excellent hearing, I overheard some rats talking about him and referring to him as Number Two."

The mice are alarmed by Murrow's revelation. Is it possible there is a new Chi Force sensitive creature out there that powerful that they don't know about? "This is very interesting and frightening," Knyse said to Murrow. "We will let our Grandmaster know about this when we see him next week." The mice then thank Murrow for sharing his information with them and went on their way.

The mice went further into the wooded area to wait for the sun to set. Autumn sunsets in Central Park when the fall foliage is at its peak are spectacular. The willow trees here turn the most vibrant shades of orange and yellow imaginable. The mice parked themselves on a small grassy mound overlooking a hill blanketed by fallen orange and golden yellow leaves. The setting sun cast long glowing shadows while the mice sat quietly to enjoy the last vestiges of nice weather. The picturesque romantic scene is a photographer's dream. As the full moon appeared in the evening sky, the mice felt a surge of Chi Energy go through their little bodies. They began to stretch as one might do first thing in the morning upon waking up. The mice then began to grow in size. Transforming from pint sized rodents to human sized ninjas.

In their enlarged form, the mice were eager to try their powers. With each full moon or **planetary alignment** in the solar system, the Ninja Mice's Chi Energy powers and abilities are enhanced or altered. Enhanced and altered abilities are usually temporary in nature and they go away with the disappearing full moon. But grandmasters like Greenspan can retain and summon enhanced and altered abilities without a full moon. Overall, however, enhanced and altered abilities are usually relatively weak. They are limited and **proportional** to an Asumari's training and sensitivity to the Chi Force.

"Look what I can do!!!" Buffy shouted as smoke and fog formed around him to conceal his exact location. "I can make smoke and fog appear! And I can control them too!"

"That's awesome, Buffy!" Knyse cheered as he began to test his abilities. He soon discovered he could create small electrostatic discharges that radiated from his body. They resembled streams of miniature lightning sparks emitting from a plasma ball. It was visually impressive, but not lethal in any sense. But then suddenly a fierce wind began to blow. The trees swayed back and forth and leaves flew in the wind. The sky then rumbled and cracked with the sound of large lightning sparks. "Whoa! That wasn't me," Knyse shouted. "Was that you, René?"

"Yeah, I think so!" René answered. "I think I can control the wind and the weather," he continued as he directed wind to blow in the direction of Buffy. "There you are! I see you now, Buffy. What about you, Soros? What can you do?" René asked.

When the full moon appeared in the sky, Soros felt stronger than he had even been. His strength compelled him to walk over to a nearby boulder his size and he was able to pick it up over his head. Soros soon discovered that he could also hold it up with his Chi Force powers alone. **"Look guys, no hands!"** proclaimed Soros.

"Wow, that's so awesome!" Knyse shouted excitedly. "I think I know how the full moon is affecting our powers tonight," he continued. "It's related to who we are naturally," he explained. "Soros is naturally a big strong guy. The full moon is making him even stronger. René, you are fast like the wind and lightning quick. And me, I have a hot temper and sparkling personality. But I'm not sure about Buffy and his smoke and fog."

"I know, I know!" René chimed in. "Buffy is naturally gassy!!! That was you who farted at yoga yesterday, wasn't it?!! Admit it!!!"

"No it wasn't," Buffy denied. "And I told you my farts don't stink! They smell like the pastries I eat," he joked as everyone shared in the laughs. "And speaking of eating, let's go over to Jeremy's!!!"

The mice made their way out from Central Park and across town over to **Jeremy the Jerk** – a Jamaican jerk chicken restaurant named after its owner. Jeremy is a human friend of the Ninja Mice. His Michelin rated restaurant is very popular and well known for its fusion cuisine and use of curry and spices. Jerk is a style of cooking native to Jamaica in which meat is dry rubbed with very hot spice mixture called Jamaican Jerk Spice. Arriving at the restaurant, the mice are greeted warmly by their old friend, Jeremy. They don't see each other as often as they like. Jeremy is always busy running his very successful restaurant. And the mice? Well, they're busy being ninjas, saving the world or helping others. The mice are seated at a quiet part of the restaurant with a little more privacy.

"What can I get for you kids tonight?" asked Jeremy. Because it was food Friday, the mice were open to trying anything. Jeremy suggested chicken roti, a dish rich in spices, chickpeas and potato – an incredible meal that he thought would excite their taste buds. The mice were all eager to try it, especially Buffy. And when the food came, they were not disappointed. The mice feasted like kings as they reminisced and caught up with their old friend. They told Jeremy about how their abilities had been enhanced by the full moon. Jeremy is always amazed at what the Mice can do. He asked what new aspects of the Chi Force they have learned. The mice tell him that they have learned how to temporarily pass on their Chi Growth. That means they can also make someone else grow like they grow during a full moon. But they can only do this when they are touching them. Powerful Asumari grandmasters like Greenspan can touch once and the affected individual can remain enlarged for the entire night. It was all very fascinating for Jeremy.

Their conversation was interrupted by other restaurant patrons wanting to pay for their bill. Jeremy excused himself from the table to serve the other customers. The mice witness people giving Jeremy money in exchange for their meals. They were puzzled and wondered about the concept of money. When Jeremy finished, the mice asked him, "What is money, where does it come from and why do people use it?" They also described for him how they trade for the things they need at the Flea Market in New Mouse City.

Thousands of years ago, humans lived in caves and did not use money, Jeremy explained. Our ancestors were hunters and gatherers and some were simple farmers. When they needed to eat, some would hunt for things like buffalos. If they were successful, they would eat. If not, they would starve – sometimes to death if they could not find things to pick and eat. For those that were successful at hunting and they needed other things like clothes or shoes, they would make it out of the leftover skin of the buffalo. Some hunters were very good at hunting and were successful most of the time. Others were much better at making things like clothes or tools and weapons than at hunting.

Because of these different skills and abilities, people decided that it was better to focus on what they were really good at than to try to do everything themselves. The hunter would only hunt; the craftsman would only make tools and clothes; the farmer would grow and gather food. This meant there would be more food available because hunters were better at hunting, farmers spent more time growing more food and craftsmen made more and better quality things. This is what we call specialization – to focus on producing the things we are really good at so we can make more of it. What our ancestors did every day is what we today call jobs.

When our specialized ancestors needed other things, they traded each other for it. One buffalo might be equal to 5 spears or 10 coats and 1 coat might be equal to 1 basket of food. But bringing buffalos, coats and baskets of food with you everywhere you go so you can trade when you see something you like is not very convenient or practical.

People invented money as a convenient way to trade with each other. Money can actually be anything. People who trade with each other just have to agree what they will use as money and how much things are worth. Historically, cattle, salt, grains and even seashells have been used as a form of money. We later used gold and silver as money because they can be standardized where each piece of can be made exactly the same. Historically, people have faith in gold and believe it has value because others will accept it as payment or will trade you things for it. It is only in very recent history that we started using printed paper as money. Paper money only has value because our government says it does. As long as people have faith in the power and ability of our government, people will believe paper money has value. But in many other places around the world, some people do not have faith in their country's government. Because of this, the paper money of those countries is backed by gold deposits held at a bank or by the government. That means if you take the paper money to the bank or the government, they are supposed to give you back the amount of gold it represents. So paper money, Jeremy explained, is a lot like coffee crisp chocolate bars except that it was a lot more convenient to carry around and trade with. And it doesn't expire or go bad.

The mice loved learning about the history and different forms of money from Jeremy. "Wow Jeremy, you're so smart! You should be a financial advisor," they said.

"Oh, I was. But that was in a previous life," said Jeremey. "Before I opened my restaurant, I use to work on Bay Street in Canada. Bay Street is Canada's version of Wall Street. I was an investment advisor there. It was rather boring and I didn't like my job. I'm much happier doing this."

The mice and Jeremy have been friends for a long time. But they did not know about his former life in Canada. They wondered what it must have been like as they enjoyed the last morsels of their chicken roti – savouring chunks of spicy goodness and flavour explosions. Jeremy has always given the mice delicious foods and taken care of them but this was the first time they thought about money. "Well Jeremy, we don't have any money to pay for our meal, but we do have some coffee crisp and plenty of other Halloween candies. Can we give you candy instead?" Knyse asked on behalf of everyone.

"Oh, that is so sweet of you to offer. But it's not necessary my friends," Jeremy replied. "As I always like to say, price is what you pay. Value is what you get I value our friendship. Your company is worth more to me than any amount of money or candy you could ever give me. Now who wants a second serving?"

"I thought you'd never ask!" Soros said with a relieved grin. "May I please have two more for take-away? I'm going to visit Diana and Nadia after dinner."

"It's so good, I'd love some, but I'm still working on my first." Knyse replied.

"You're such a slow eater!" René teased.

"Ummmm... How about a third serving for me?" Buffy asked sheepishly with a big greasy grin.

Jeremy was thrilled to know the mice loved the meal and wanted more. That evening, the mice were well fed. After dinner, Jeremy sent them home with a care package of extra chicken roti for everyone.

Chapter Five
Grandmaster Greenspan Returns

It was the night of Greenspan's return. Inside the darkened cabin of the **Boeing 787 Dreamliner** airplane, the human passengers were restless. It had been 12 hours since the flight departed from Japan. Most adults find it difficult to sleep on flights as seating and space are tight. But as a mouse and having his very own seat, Greenspan had plenty of legroom to stretch out and relax. In fact, Greenspan was comfortably asleep on top of an in-flight courtesy pillow and tucked under a blanket when lights began to turn on. He awoke to find the airplane cabin bathed in soft dim light and the sound of jet engines noise roaring in the background.

"Good evening, sir. Please prepare for arrival and return your chair to its upright position." said a flight attendant speaking to Greenspan. "We are making our final descent and will be landing in New York in 30 minutes."

Flight attendants and fellow passengers alike do not take notice that Greenspan is a tiny little mouse. This was likely the result of Greenspan's subtle mind control suggestion tricks when he said them, "I'm just another ordinary passenger." However, a curious child sitting in front of him looks over the headrest of her seat and back at Greenspan. "Hello, cute little mouse." she says. The child clearly sees Greenspan for who and what he is as she is not affected by his mind trick suggestion. It is likely because a child's mind is less cluttered and less distracted than grown-ups. "Did you sleep well?" she asked Greenspan.

"Hello kind little girl. Indeed, my sleep was pleasant. Sweetness, thy name is child. How art thou?" Greenspan replied in old world English with a hint of a British accent.

"You speak funny," the child said with a giggle. She was unfazed by the fact that a mouse could speak to her. Unlike adults, to a child, this was perfectly normal because no one had taught her it should be abnormal.

"I speaketh proper English," said Greenspan smiling back at the child. "I speaketh English the way I was taught by my gentleman friend, Sir William Mouspeare many years ago. My manners and habits henceforth doth have not changed," Greenspan explained to the child. They enjoyed each other's company and continued their conversation until it was time for the airplane to land.

BING... Ladies and gentlemen, it's a pleasure to welcome you to New York City. The local time is 7:20 PM. Please remain seated with your seatbelt fastened till the captain brings our airplane to a complete stop and turns off the fasten seatbelt sign. Thank you for choosing Cathay Pacific. We hope to serve you again in the near future.

Make me one with everything

After arriving, Greenspan quickly made his way out of JFK airport and onto an express train that took him down to New York Penn Station in midtown Manhattan on West 34th Street. Upon arriving at Penn Station, Greenspan was eager to make his way out to the streets of New York. He wanted to feel the energy of the big city; see its familiar sights; and smell its familiar scents. It has been over 6 months since he was last here. Once outside, Greenspan found himself standing on busy 34th Street. It was a mild evening. Night life in the big city was in full swing. City lights were bright and traffic noise was loud. A sea of yellow taxi cabs honking their horns one after another. Pedestrians and cyclists stream by at a steady pace. Evening garbage was piled up high on sidewalks in front of businesses waiting to be picked up in the wee hours of the night. Greenspan pointed his nose up to the air and inhaled deeply before letting out a sigh. The smell of city garbage, sweat, public urination and street vendor hotdogs filled the air. Some might find the overwhelming sights, sounds and aromas as an assault on the senses. But for Greenspan, it was comforting as it was all very familiar. "Ah yes, stale urine, sweaty smelly people, food carts and hotdogs... I am home!" Greenspan proclaimed.

Greenspan came back to fulfill a promise he made to his Ninja Mice pupils to help them complete their training. Before leaving the mice many months ago, Greenspan had helped them to defeat the evil mastermind, Goldmouse Sachs and his rat army. But after the battle, Greenspan needed to rest his frail body. And because he was homesick, he returned to his native Japan to recoup. Now healthy again, he has returned. After reacquainting himself with New York, Greenspan made his way down to Wall Street. There, he went into the tunnel connecting Wall Street to New Mouse City and towards the Ninja Mice dojo. As Greenspan got closer, he could feel the familiar Chi Energy of the Ninja Mice. The mice also felt his presence approaching the dojo. As the dojo door swung open, Greenspan was greeted by a loud cheering eruption of "**WELCOME HOME!!!**" The Ninja Mice and a few friends were there to welcome Greenspan home.

There was Nadia and Diana, long-time friends of the Ninja Mice and admirers of Grandmaster Greenspan. Not only are Nadia and Diana roommates, they are also the co-owners of United Candy Nations – a fancy store specializing in candies from around the world that are made to look like jewels. For example, cherry flavoured lollipops and green apple flavoured candies that look like rubies and emeralds. Nadia is the hardworking brains behind the operation. She's a perfectionist with an eye for detail. Nadia tends to be a bit nerdy and strive for a perfect 10 in everything she does. Diana on the other hand is the face and the marketing genius of the operation. She is the more relaxed and easy-going of the two roommates and business partners. Diana is a girly girl with grace and social skills who tends to be a bit of a princess – always wanting the best and expecting the best, but also giving the best. The girls are great friends and work well together. Upon seeing the girls, Greenspan greeted them warmly. He brought back special candies for them that you can only find in Japan.

Also there for the homecoming were two grumpy old rodents named **Mao** and **Shek**. These two are more like grateful admirers than close friends of the Ninja Mice and Greenspan. Mao and Shek are rival business owners that don't normally get along. But for this evening, they put aside their differences to help welcome Greenspan home. Mao, a grumpy old chubby mouse with a receding hairline, runs Chairman Mao's Furniture Store which specializes in chairs. Shek, a grumpy old thin mouse with a mustache, runs Shek's KMT Store. KMT is a household furnishing shop that sells knives, mattresses and tables.

The location of the Ninja Mice dojo is a secret and only a few know where it is or how to find it. The two rivals, Mao and Shek are there to show their appreciation. Greenspan and the Ninja Mice saved their furniture stores from burning down during the epic battle with Goldmouse over a year ago. Because of their actions, Mao and Shek each generously gave Greenspan and the Ninja Mice all the furnishing they needed for their Dojo. Almost everything you see in the dojo – all the furnishing, decorations, interior design and **feng-shui** layout – was courtesy of Mao and Shek. And because they personally delivered the furniture to the Ninja Mice, Mao and Shek know the secret location of the dojo. Although they are long-time rivals, Mao and Shek should be natural allies. Their businesses are actually complimentary as they do not compete directly with each other. Because of this, they have talked about merging their two companies together into one. But neither can ever agree on how or who should run the resulting combined company. Sadly, they just don't know how to get along. They should really get advice from Nadia and Diana on how to work well with others.

Lastly in attendance was Lafayette, a charming aristocratic friend of the Ninja Mice. Because of his long name, everyone just calls him **L**. Before meeting Grandmaster Greenspan and the Ninja Mice, Lafayette was under the control of Goldmouse Sachs and his rat army. L is the owner of **Gilbert's** – a fancy French café shop where you can find the best cheeses, macarons, baguettes, wines, croissants and escargots – and **The GENERAL Store** where you can find all sorts of army-surplus and knick-knacks for your home. Under Goldmouse's control, L was forced to feed the rats for free whenever they showed up at his café. And they would also take whatever they wanted from his Store. L came to the homecoming celebration to show his appreciate for the time the Ninja Mice and Grandmaster Greenspan freed him from Goldmouse's control. Ever since the rats were beaten up, they have never bothered L again. To show his appreciation, L brought over all the best French treats imaginable – including a Prime wedge of **Stenchbrick blue cheese**, which everyone enjoyed while holding their noses. When it comes to blue cheese, the saying is: the stinkier the better! The Stenchbrick, however, is on a whole other level. Its odor is like forgotten sweaty gym socks left at the bottom of a laundry basket underneath a pile of wet vinegar rags that were used to wipe up the week-old Russian potato salad that you vomited. **EEEW!** Fumes from the Stenchbrick pack quite a punch as it can burn through your nasal mucous membranes if inhaled deeply from the source. Prolonged exposure can lead to **hallucinations** and loss of short term memory... It's hell on your nose, but heaven in your mouth. Stenchbricks are sure tasty. And they sure are stinky too! **PHEW.**

Everyone at the party was surprised and delighted by the sight of the special blue cheese. Stenchbricks are referred to as **Prime** when they are made with the very best ingredients and are packaged very carefully. When they are made with inferior or expired ingredients and are handled and aged poorly, they are referred to as **Subprime**. Considered toxic, this addictive blue cheese is oh so irresistibly delicious and popular. So much so that it use to trade on the Mouse International Cheese Exchange (**MICE**). There was even a market index developed around it called the Morgan Stinky Cheese Index (**MSCI**). But the once plentiful Stenchbrick has become very scarce in recent times. Because of lack of supply, it is no longer traded on the MICE

Market. No one knows for sure what exactly happened to the supply of Stenchbricks. Many have speculated the makers of blue cheese may have developed brain damage due to long term exposure to the noxious fumes. There are also rumours that someone is stealing the cheese and hoarding it somewhere, to hungry rats eating it all... no one knows for sure. The small wedge of Stenchbrick that Lafayette brought came from his personal inventory which he was saving for a special occasion.

French cheese can be divided into three main families:
1. **Pressed Cheeses** (also known as Hard)
2. **Soft Cheeses** (such as Brie and Camembert)
3. **Blue Cheeses** (varies widely from bland to sharp)

They are traditionally made from three types of milk (cow, goat or sheep) and can come from either a farmhouse or an industrial manufacturer.

Greenspan was overjoyed to see everyone at the dojo. The feeling was of course mutual. Food and drinks were abundant. Aside from the all the French treats brought by Lafayette, Buffy made gourmet thin crust pizza and sushi. Mao and Shek each brought loads of fruits and drinks. Nadia and Diana brought boxes of chocolates to share. Greenspan brought back with him souvenir and gifts for everyone as it was his habit whenever he traveled. For his Ninja Mice, Greenspan got them something very special – rare Japanese Pokémon collector cards and hand-made **Shurikens** (commonly known as throwing stars).

The homecoming celebration continued late into the night and well past everyone's bedtime. When the time finally came for everyone to go home, Lafayette, being the well-mannered charming gentlemouse that he was, walked Nadia and Diana home. The Ninja Mice got ready for bed by brushing their teeth and changing into their pajamas. But despite the late hour, the mice could not fall asleep. This was likely because they were too excited and happy to see their Grandmaster again... That, and probably all the **After Eight** chocolate they ate. The caffeine in those things will keep most mice bouncing off the walls well past midnight. As the mice could not sleep, Greenspan agreed to read them a bedtime story. The book they selected was a classic children's book, **Guess How Much I Love You.** As all the lights in the dojo were turned off, Greenspan read to the mice with a flashlight.

Little Nutbrown Hare, who was going to bed, held on tight to Big Nutbrown Hare's very long ears. Greenspan read... But by the time he got to the end, Then he lay down close by and whispered with a smile, "*I love you right up to the moon – and back.*" the mice were still awake. Everyone laid quietly in the dark while Greenspan waited for them to fall asleep.

"Why did you go to Japan?" Knyse asked quietly. "What's it like there?" As is often the case at the end of the day, the mice tend to ask deep philosophical questions and ponder about the future and meaning of life. At bedtime when the activities and energy levels are calmer, the mice are more introspective. Sometimes they think of all the problems in the world. And when they do, it can feel like the weight of the world is resting on their shoulders.

Grandmaster explained to the Ninja Mice that Japan is a place like no other. It is a place where the ultra-high-tech modern world is harmoniously balanced with the simple traditional ways of life. It is a prosperous society where ancient Buddhist shrines bump up against skyscrapers. Temples and palaces whisper of history and bullet trains shuttle you through spectacular landscapes to cities packed with world-class restaurants and shops. In Japanese society, one's honour and respect, especially for family and elders, are of utmost importance. And everyone is always courteous and respectful – even in big cities. Mousaka, for example, is very safe and quiet considering it is one of the biggest cities in the world and second largest in Japan with 20 million inhabitants living within a 10,000 tail radius from its center. Quietness, politeness and respectful behaviour are deeply entrenched in the Japanese psyche. It is not feigned or cynically observed; it is a sincere and genuine sensibility, a core value of the society. Bowing is a common practice, too, but it is not a cultural cliché, cynically performed, but rather a universal gesture of respect. Space is limited and highly valued. They believe in the notion of quality over quantity; simplicity devoid of unnecessary elements. The Japanese are also hardworking and incredibly precise. Their meticulous and careful nature is reflected in every aspect of daily life. From trains that run right on time to food preparation to the craftsmanship in the things they build. The katana, a razor sharp sword made of hardened carbon steel folded many thousands of times and wrapped around a soft flexible core, is the embodiment of their strive for perfection. Hard work is a way of life and is evidenced by sleep deprived commuters who are often sleeping, even while standing up, in packed trains.

For Grandmaster Greenspan, Japan is his first home. It was a place he missed badly and needed to revisit and reconnect with. But for the Ninja Mice, New Mouse City is the only home they have ever known. It is the only place they've ever lived in so it was hard for them to really understand what it means to miss home. Grandmaster described home as the place where your heart is – the place where your friends and family are. It is the place where you grow up wanting to leave, and grow old wanting to get back to. It is all the things that are familiar and makes you feel warm inside. Home is a place where you can visit the days that have passed; to see how far you've come and how much you've grown.

"Grandmaster, what happens to all the days that have gone?" René asked quietly under his breath as he began to drift off.

"Methinks they art still with us," said Greenspan "In ye memories and life experience."

"Who taught you about the Chi Force and trained you to be an Asumari?" Soros asked.

"**Madiba** was the one who traineth me. That gent was a wise and powerful Asumari who lived in South Africa. He discovered me when I was there on a safari trip. And **Gundi** was his master before that. Many consider Gundi as the wisest of all Asumari Grandmasters in history.

"Grandmaster," Knyse interrupted. "We've heard reports there might be a new and very powerful Asumari in town. His name may be Merrill Pynch and he doesn't sound very friendly." Knyse continued. The mice then explained to their grandmaster all the things Merrill Pynch was capable of doing as told to them by Murrow the owl. But Greenspan was not fazed by the news of the new potential threat in town.

"I hadst a **premonition** while I was recuperating in Japan about this Merrill Pynch character," Greenspan explained to his Ninja Mice. "In mine own dream state, I did see a powerful monster commanding an army of thousands of rats; allied with snakes; enslaving millions of mice; and feeding us mice to the snakes."

"That's awful!" Buffy shrieked.

"Indeed tis awful. But premonitions art not the future. They are only what may happen if thou doth not act. That is why I cameth back earlier than I hadst planned. I must prepareth thee to face Merrill Pynch."

"But Grandmaster, what if we are not strong enough to take him on?" Knyse inquired nervously. "What if he's even more powerful than we thought?"

"Thy body doth what thy mind believeth possible. Thou shall never defeat thy enemy only because thou believeth true. If thou shall only do what thou can do, thou shall never be more than thou art now."

The Ninja Mice laid quietly in the dark and thought about the words of their Grandmaster. They realized he was right. It is true that you can do whatever you truly believe is possible. The only reason something is impossible is because you believe it is true. And if you never push yourself to do more; if you only do the things you're capable of doing, then you will never be more than what you are now. "How will we know when we are ready to take on Merrill Pynch?" The mice asked Greenspan.

"In the morning, ye shall search for this Merrill Pynch. But now ye must rest and sleep while I teach what ye must know in order to defeat even the most powerful of enemies. To be a fully trained

Asumari Ninja, ye must know all of the following." Greenspan said as he outlined the main principles of the Asumari ways.

Know Your Power and Self

With great powers comes great responsibility. An Asumari must use his powers wisely, proportionately and only when necessary. It would be unwise for one to use a hammer when he seeks to swat a mosquito from his nose. Thus, ye shall save thy powers for when it shall be truly necessary. It will be tempting to use your powers frivolously and on many occasions. Sometimes it will be for vanity, for selfish gains or simply to cheat and win against a lesser opponent. For example it would be unethical to read a rival's thoughts to win money from him in a game of cards. Ye shall not take advantage of the weak. Do onto others as you would have others do onto you. An Asumari must only use his powers for good and every action he takes must come from a good place in his heart.

Know Your Skills

Speed, agility and instincts matter just as much as strength. No matter the size or strength of your enemy, he cannot hit what is not there. Stealth and shadow are your allies. The ninja who strikes in silence can overcome an army alone. But thou shall know only defeat if thou makes a squeak and betray thy location before thou art ready. Thus a skilled ninja can defeat a stronger opponent or an entire army by using his natural skills to evade detection and strikes.

Know Your Enemy

You may know your skills, have mastered every ninja fighting technique or even control all the Chi Force in the universe, but are you a master of your foe? You must study him, understand his drives and motivations, think as he thinks and feel as he feels. To know thy enemy is to know thyself. To know thy enemy, thou must become thy enemy and thou shall be able to predict thy enemy's moves. This means if you know your enemy and you know your skills, in a 1000 battles, you will not be in danger.

Know Your Land

Ye shall be keenly observant of thy surroundings. A ninja must be one with his environment and the battle field he is on. That means knowing where the shadows will fall at any given time, knowing which direction the wind is likely to blow and where an enemy might easily hide. It means seeing that a rock, a tree limb or a book are not just decorative features of your surroundings, but potential weapons. Always take the high ground in battle and have the sun to your back so that it is in your enemy's eyes.

The Art of War

Once you have mastered what you must know, you must then apply your learning. In all battles, a Ninja shall use the art of deception to his advantage. This means, when you are strong, act weak. This will entice your enemy to attack. When you are weak, act strong. This shall deter your enemy from attacking. When glorious and victorious, be humble and kind. Otherwise you invite hatred, jealousy or envy that can motivate your enemies to plot against you. The supreme art of war is to subdue your enemy without fighting. When you can do this, you are then a fully trained Asumari. The highest honour for an Asumari would be to turn an enemy into a friend.

Chapter Six
Goldmouse and the Chocolate Factory

The morning after Grandmaster Greenspan's return, the Ninja Mice headed out to find the rumoured Merrill Pynch. Not knowing if the menacing figure was real or fiction, the mice went to places where rats are known to frequent. Their first stop was **Smells Kitchen** – a gritty midtown section of New Mouse City along the Hudson River. The area once had a cooking school and a thriving restaurant scene where aspiring young chefs apply their skills. But due to economic recessions, many, including the school, have moved out. The area is now a haven for criminals and thieves. Shady characters like weasels, snakes and wannabe gangsters have moved in looking for an easy meal.

The main access point in and out of Smells Kitchen is **Stinken Tunnel**. Walking around Smells Kitchen, Knyse felt apprehensive and was on constant alert. Using his Chi Force, he could feel he and his friends were being watched. Big strong Soros and fearless René weren't bothered or concerned at all. Buffy on the other hand was too oblivious as he was more concerned about finding a decent place for lunch. Food was never far from his mind. **SNIFF SNIFF SNIFF…** "I can't find anything decent. The only thing I smell around here is the desperation… Desperation for real food." said Buffy.

"Stay focused, Buffy! We're here to find Merrill Pynch, not Merrill Lunch." said Knyse.

Suddenly, a sinister voice calls out to the Ninja Mice. "What are you mice doing here?!" an unfriendly voice asked rhetorically. It was an eastern garter snake hiding in the shadows. "You better get outta here before you get hurt," he warned.

Buffy and Soros simply smiled and said "Hello. Good morning. How are you, Mr. Snake?"

"We're here looking for someone," Knyse chimed in. "We're looking for..." but before he could finish what he was saying, the snake slid away.

"Okay, nice talking to you. Have a nice day." René said sarcastically. This was immediately followed by Knyse, Soros and Buffy saying: "**Nnnnnno, not nice. N-eeeeyes talking to ya!**"

"And it was Knyse that was talking to you." they tried to explain to the snake, but he was long gone by then.

Suddenly, a desperate scream came from a distant up ahead. "**Help! Help!**" Someone yelled. The Ninja Mice ran towards the distress call for help. It was a young girl being attacked by a large rat. "Stop right there!" Soros yelled at the rat as the Ninja Mice charged at him. In a panic, the rat released the young girl who instinctively fled as soon as he let go. The rat also fled, but in the opposite direction. The Ninja Mice chased after him. But after a few seconds of running, the rat realized he was being chased by much smaller mice. He stopped and decided to turn around to face his pursuers instead.

"Why don't you pick on someone your own size, you jerk!" said Soros to the rat.

"Pick on someone my own size, eh?" said the rat. "You referring to yourselves? Cuz I don't see anyone my size. All I see is a bunch of pipsqueaks. I'll take on all of you myself." The rat taunted.

"It won't take all of us to defeat you, rat. The big guy here can take you on all by himself." Knyse said referring to Soros.

"What, that's not fair!" René jokingly objected. "Why does Soros get to have all the fun? I want to beat up the rat too!"

"**GRRRR!**" the rat snarled and growled. He picked up a discarded pipe that was on the ground and charged at Soros. But the big guy was ready for him and stood his ground. The rat was half a tail length taller than Soros. He swung the metal pipe down like it was a hammer at Soros who was like the nail he was trying to hit. Soros easily side stepped the blow causing the rat to hit the concrete ground instead. The shock of metal hitting concrete sent a violent jolt up the rat's right arm causing him to drop the pipe. He clutched his right arm with his left hand in severe pain. Soros looked at the rat with disdain. He knew that despite his bigger size, the rat was no match for him. At this point, Soros simply took his Bo Staff and wacked it across the rat's shins causing him to fall to his knees. René then stepped up to the rat.

"Well, looks like you're almost my size now. So I guess it's my turn, huh?" René taunted. "Tell me Mr. Rat, are you hungry? You fancy a sandwich? Because I've got a knuckle sandwich here for you..." **POW!** René hits the rat with a thunderous uppercut lifting him up off his knees. The rat fell backwards. Realizing he was out numbered and outmatched, the rat crawled away with his tail between his legs.

"You've beaten me this time. But I'm going to get my friends and you'll be sorry then." The rat whimpered defiantly.

"Okay Mr. Rat. Have a nice day. Tell your friends the Ninja Mice said hi." Buffy said in a sincere and genuine tone. "By the way, do you or your friends know anyone named Merrill Pynch? Oh, and also, do you know a good place to eat around here?" The rat did not look or answer back and kept on crawling away.

The Ninja Mice went on their way further and deeper into Smells Kitchen. They encountered many more local residents. Most of them were low level street thugs who were either indifferent to the mice's inquiries or too afraid to talk. As the mice continued to wander the streets of Smells Kitchen, Knyse got the sense he and his friends were being followed. He and the rest of the Ninja Mice decided to turn into a dark alley to see if whoever was behind them would follow. Moments later, a sound came from in front of them of a garbage can tipping over. The mice stopped in their tracks. From the dark corner in front of them, a gang of five massive rats emerged from the shadows. Standing in the middle was a rat at least a full tail length taller than Soros. Smoking a nasty cigarette, he appeared to be the gang leader so the mice thought of him as Boss Rat. He was flanked by four other rats. Three of them were about half a tail length taller than Soros while the fourth was about the same size as the big Ninja Mice.

"That's them!" a voice from behind the Ninja Mice shouted. It was the mugger rat whom the ninjas beat up earlier. And it was him who was following the mice all along. "Those are the mice that jumped me and mugged me when I wasn't looking. They got the better of me because I was unarmed."

"What are you talking about?!! Are you on drugs or something? Have you lost your mind?" Knyse countered. "You tried to attack us after you tried to mug a defenseless little girl. You deserved the beating we gave you."

"I don't care what he did or didn't do." said Boss Rat. "I'm Killer Karl the Rat and we are the Nabisco Gang. Around here the rule is, if you beat up one of our guys, we put one of yours in the hospital. If you put one of ours in the hospital, we put one of yours in the grave. So get ready for what's coming."

Knyse and the rest of the Ninja Mice were not impressed or felt threatened. "You sure you guys want to do this?" Knyse asked. And as he did, he could sense the shorter rat that was the same size as Soros was very nervous and scared. Knyse decided to use his powers to influence his thoughts. "Shorty, you don't want any part of this." Knyse projected.

The short rat in the group then said out loud, "I don't want any part of this." The other rats all turned to looked at him. They were stunned.

"You want to go home. It's a school night. You have homework and you need to do laundry." Knyse continued.

"I want to go home. It's a school night. I have homework and laundry to do. See you later guys." Shorty said walking away.

"What the heck?!!" Boss Rat mumbled. "Okay fine. So it'll be a five-on-four fight then."

"Uh, no. It's a three-on-one fight." Knyse correcting Boss Rat.

"How do you figure that? Did you fail math and you don't know how to count or something?" Boss Rat asked smugly.

"Well, first of all, my friend Buffy here is not really interested in fighting." Knyse clarified. "He hasn't had lunch yet and he would rather go grab a bite if you want to join him. Second, my little buddy René here is going to fight on behalf of all of us. So that's one on our side. You're the leader of the gang so you have to start the fight. But once your gang sees our smallest guy take out your biggest guy, that's you by the way Mr. Boss Rat, two of your overly enthusiastic henchrats will jump in to join the fun. So that makes three on your side. But once René beats up all 3 on your side, Mugger will realize he doesn't want to go a second round and get beat up by René again. Your final guy will see Mugger run like a chicken and three of his friends just got beat up by a tiny pipsqueak. He'll then realize that he should also go home to do homework and laundry as well. Now do you get why this is a three-on-one fight?"

As Knyse laid out the sequence of events and how the fight would unfold, he knew Boss Rat could not back down from the challenge put forth to him. As the leader and biggest member of the gang, Boss Rat would look cowardly if he backed down from a fight with a tiny mouse a third his size. His followers would lose respect and fear of him. They would no longer think he was cool or tough. Boss Rat's ego forced him to step up and fight René.

"Enough!" Boss rat snarled. He charged at René who in return ran towards Boss Rat with Tonfas in his hands to meet him half way. Boss Rat swung his fists wildly at René over and over again, missing each time. Trying to hit René was like trying to punch a mosquito or grab smoke. You can't hit or grab what is not there. It just can't be done. After trying a dozen times of swinging and missing, Boss Rat was out of breath; huffing and puffing.

"Had enough yet, Bossy?" René taunted. Boss Rat took a moment to catch his breath before winding up to throw his hardest and fastest punch yet. As the punch came, René decided not to side step the blow this time. Instead, he wound up to throw his own punch with the Tonfa in his hand. Boss Rat's fist collided violently with the point of René's Tonfa shattering the bones in his hand. The intense pain immediately registered in Boss Rat's brain as he cradled his broken hand in agony. René then sprung up in the air with a devastating spinning kick to Boss Rat's face knocking him unconscious.

Immediately following this, and as Knyse predicted, two of the henchrats rushed René. One tried to spear tackle him around the waist. But René met him with a flying knee to his face. The second henchrat was more successful. As René was dealing with the first henchrat, the second one managed to blindside him with a hard punch to side of his face. René was staggered. The second henchrat then pulled out a thick heavy metal chain weapon the length of his tail. He swung it wildly at René's head who barely ducked in time. The second henchrat swung it again and again. René had to jump or duck each time to avoid the thick heavy chain. He was starting to get tired from all ducking and jumping. The next swing that came at him, René decided he would block the chain with his forearm which was guarded by the shaft of his Tonfa. As the chain came around again, René held up high his left arm and Tonfa to protect his head. He blocked the chain as he anticipated, but it wrapped around his arm and Tonfa causing it come around to hit him in the back of the head. René fell to his hands and knees. He was hurt. The henchrat saw his opportunity to finish the fight. He whipped the chain weapon downwards as hard as he could at René. But René was able to roll out of the way. The Henchrat missed completely. The heavy chain struck the concrete ground forcefully instead, causing it to bounce back at the Henchrat, hitting him in the face. He was dazed. René then saw his opening and swung his Tonfa like a baseball bat at his adversary, hitting him on the side of the head, knocking the henchrat out cold.

The third henchrat, who was up to this point only watching the fight and waiting for his chance to jump in, looked over to his friend, the Mugger rat. In that moment, they both decided that homework and laundry sounded pretty good right about then and fled the scene. Just then, the first henchrat that was knocked down by René's flying knee earlier started to regain his senses. Knyse grabbed him by the collar and said, "We weren't looking for any trouble."

"Nope," echoed Buffy. "We were just looking for a guy named Merrill Pynch... that and also lunch. Know a good place to eat around here?"

"I'm not telling you anything. He'll kill me if I say anything!" The henchrat rambled.

"Who will kill you?" Knyse inquired. "Who are you afraid of? Tell me now or I will feed you to a snake."

"Okay. Okay... I don't know his real name. I only know he's called number two by some of the rats who work for him. He's called that because he works for someone else. I don't know who. But one of my friends who work for him gave me this..." The henchrat pulls out a chocolate morsel wrapped in gold tinfoil. "I was going to eat it, but you can have it. And that's all I know. I swear!"

Knyse sensed he was truthful. But before letting him go, Knyse wanted the henchrat to pass on a message. "Tell all your criminal friends to not mess with the Ninja Mice. Because when you mess with the best, you die like the rest!" With that said, the henchrat scurried away. Having found a clue to the existence of Merrill Pynch, the mice always went on their way.

As the Ninja Mice left the scene, René was still a little wobbly but otherwise okay after the fight. He asked Knyse, "How did you know I would be able to defeat those rats all by myself?"

"I didn't." Knyse replied. "But I had faith in your abilities. If you would have gotten into serious trouble, we would have stepped in. I just thought we had to try our fighting skills. But the fact that you did manage to defeat them all on your own enhances our reputation. If you, as a tiny little pipsqueak, are this powerful and dangerous on your own… can you imagine how powerful and deadly we would be if all four of us were fighting? Those rats are going to tell their friends. We'll be legendary! No one in Smells Kitchen will ever dare to attack us with our reputation. That's the supreme art of war! Subdue your enemy without fighting!"

"I completely agree, Knyse." said Buffy. "But if we had taken them out for lunch, they might have become friends too… That's the ultimate honour!"

As the Ninja Mice continued to track down leads, across town at the United Candy Nations shop, Nadia and Diana are having a busy day as usual. The girls are proud of the successful business they've built together. Stocked with the sweetest and most fancy candies from all over the world, the shop is quite popular with mouselets and girls. Their most popular items include rock sugar that look like crystals and white diamonds, ruby lollipops, green apple emeralds and grape flavoured amethysts. Boys are seldom seen in the shop unless it's a special occasion like Valentine's Day – a day when boys tend to give something fancy and pretty for the special ladies in their lives.

Diana was standing behind the counter while Nadia was helping a group of young girls pick out the perfect set of gumball pearls when a tall dark stranger walked into the shop. The stranger was a gruff and disheveled looking male rat wearing a hoodie and dark sunglasses. He was sweaty, covered in chocolate stains, looking nervous and completely out of place. Nadia noticed him right away. She was confused for a moment and thought to herself, "Was it Christmas already? Is it Valentine's Day today?" but quickly realized it wasn't. She then thought, "What does he want here? Does he want to use the washroom or something?" Nadia then realized she was behaving terribly as she was judging the rat and forming negative opinions based on his appearance.

"Welcome to United Candy Nations sir!" said Nadia with a warm and genuine smile. "How can I help you?"

The rat was surprised by Nadia's warmth and friendliness that it made him even more nervous for what he was about to do. Not knowing what to do next or how else to respond, he simply mumbled, "Uh, I'm looking for stuff."

"Well, we have got plenty of those." Nadia joked. "Was there anything in particular you were looking for? And is it for yourself or for a special friend?" Nadia inquired.

"Uh, I'm looking for... uh, your best looking... uh, your most realistic looking jewel candies. Something like THIS!" The rat growled and pointed at the gumball pearls in hands of the young girls whom Nadia was helping a moment ago. He then snatched the gumball pearls violently from the young girls. The girls cowed in fear as the rat towered over them. Nadia's friendly disposition turned to shock and disappointment with rat's lack of manners. She grabbed the pearls out the rat's hand which distracted his attention from the girls. The terrorised girls and other customers used the opportunity to scurry away and run out the shop. Nadia was furious with the rat's behaviour at this point and was ready to throttle him for scaring away her customers.

From behind the counter, Diana chimed in to intervene hoping to salvage the situation "Oh, Mr. Rat, could I interest you in some diamonds or emeralds or amethyst? They're quite pretty and popular." She said cheerfully. The rat walked over to Diana at the counter while Nadia stood by the door seething.

"Yes, I'm interested in all of them. Show me everything you've got!" The rat ordered. Diana was not offended or put off by the rat's obvious rudeness. Instead, she invited the rat sit and have tea with her while she showed him samples. She even offered him a special Japanese mint candy to go along with his tea. It was the same ones that were given to her by Greenspan just last night. Diana hoped that by being kind, the rat would less hostile and rude. She believed in showing kindness and love to others even when they don't necessarily deserve it. Because those who least deserve it are often the ones who need it the most.

The rat sipped his tea as Diana pulled out box after box of jewel candies which sparkled brightly. She tried to explain to the rat how each one taste and where they come from. But the rat was impatient, "Okay, yeah, yeah, yeah. Show me the next one. Go!" As Diana pulled out another box from the display case, the rat suddenly and without warning, threw his tea in Diana's face. She was stunned. The rat then shoved Diana away from the counter and quickly grabbed as many boxes as he could hold and ran for the door. He could barely see where he was going. The boxes were stacked up to his nose.

As the rat headed for the exit, Nadia was still standing near the door. She stuck her foot out as he ran passed causing him to trip. The rat crashed chin first to the ground and sparkling candy went flying everywhere. He was momentarily dazed, but it was enough to allow Nadia to jump on his back. She grabbed the rat by the neck and began choking him with the gumball pearls she had in her hands. Diana quickly joined in, punching him in the back of the head at first and then kicking him. "**How dare you! How dare you!**" She screamed. But soon, the rat regained his senses. He used his size and strength advantage to push his way up and managed to pull Nadia off his back and throw her across the room. The rat then turned his focus to Diana, who at the point feared for her life. As he wound up for a big punch, Nadia jumped across the room with a flying kick to the back of the rat's head, causing him to tumble forward towards Diana as she braced for impact. But in an instant, Diana also saw her opportunity – a boy's ultimate weakness... his private parts. With fire in her eyes, Diana kicked the rat right between the legs like a determined footballer needing to score a goal. **K-POW!** The rat stopped dead in his tracks. His face frozen motionless and his mouth gaped open. There was a brief moment of complete silence in the store before rat's expressionless face turned into a look of agony. It was followed by an ear shattering scream of pain. **YAA-AGH!** The rat fell to his knees. Then he hit the ground face first. Laying facedown his stomach and clutching his private parts in pain, the rat inched his way out of the shop by pushing with his hind legs.

"**How dare you try to steal from us?!! We were nice to you! Get outta here and don't ever come back!**" They yelled.

Meanwhile in an industrial part of uptown New York, there were signs of activity at an old chocolate factory. The factory was once the biggest and busiest chocolate manufacturing facility in the world. But the company that owned it went bankrupt and the factory had not been used in many years. The building itself was old and crumbly and surrounded by overgrown weeds. From the outside, the factory looked dilapidated and abandoned. But on the inside, it was anything but abandoned. In the basement level extending into New Mouse City, the old factory was filled with thousands of rats working on an assembly line. The rats all wore uniforms with some appearing to be officers or supervisors while others appeared to be lowly subordinates. They are working furiously and with military precision to produce chocolate. In one corner of the factory, there was a massive fountain. The fountain is the reservoir where molten chocolate is stored before it is processed and molded into individual treats.

High above in a dimly lit room overlooking the factory floor was an office. Inside was the mysterious and menacing Merrill Pynch. He is on a video conference call with Goldmouse Sachs who is at an undisclosed location. Goldmouse is actually a rat but he is so small that everyone thinks he is a mouse. His diminutive size makes him bitter and angry. He compensates his small stature by always wearing gold and a business suit or a shirt, tie and vest. Goldmouse is an evil sinister criminal mastermind who is always plotting to take over the world. His ultimate goal is to rule the world making everyone a slave or employee of his criminal business empire working for minimal wage. Goldmouse is very strong with the Chi Force and is an Asumari. He was last seen more than a year ago when he was involved in an epic battle with the Ninja Mice. Goldmouse lost that battle and since then has been in hiding in his new head office – a lavish suite decorated with gold and marble, accented by a **Commode on Legs**. He is hiding there with his personal assistant, **Volentina Tereshkova**. An accomplished assassin, Volentina is Goldmouse's bodyguard, chauffeur and pilot. He calls her **Tina** for short. Only a few in the criminal underworld know Goldmouse survived the epic battle and is still alive.

Merrill Pynch on the other hand is a new disciple of Goldmouse and even fewer know of his existence. He is dressed in traditional samurai armour more for visual intimidation than for protection. But his red bladed katana can do more than just intimidate. It is a lethal sword infused with his own blood to make the razor sharp blade red. Although not much is known about Merrill Pynch at this point, what is clear is he is physically imposing. When he growls and shows off his teeth, Merrill looks more like a wolf than a rat. If looks could kill, you'd be dead already. In Merrill's office, he and Goldmouse are having a conference call update. A hologram image of Goldmouse is projected high on the wall in the dimly lit room. Merrill is bowed down on one knee.

Merrill: "What is thy command my master?"

Goldmouse: "You have grown strong and powerful with the Chi Force my apprentice."

Merrill: "It is all because of you, my master. You saved my life and gave me purpose and the means to unleash my anger. You have made me everything that I am. For that, I am your loyal servant."

Goldmouse: "How are the plans coming along?"

Merrill: "Everything is on schedule, master. We should have a million chocolate gold coins and bars by the end of the week."

Goldmouse: "Excellent. What about the **counterfeit** money?"

Merrill: "The printers that were used to print the candy wrappers have been converted to print counterfeit money. And instead of using candy wrapper paper, we are using **Panama Papers** to print the counterfeit money as you ordered."

Goldmouse: "Good. Now what about plans for the diamonds and precious gem stones?"

Merrill: "I sent one of our new recruits to collect candy replicas from the United Candy Nations store. He should be back soon."

Goldmouse: "Excellent! We will be ready to strike soon. And this time, the Ninja Mice will not stop be able to stop us! Carry on."

As soon as Merrill's conference call ends, there was a knock on his door. It was the rat who tried to rob the United Candy Nations store. He looked very nervous and afraid. Trembling and unable to speak, Merrill knew immediately he had failed the mission.

"You let a couple of little mice girls beat you up?!!" Merrill screamed as he drew his Katana. "You have failed me for the last time!" But instead of striking the new recruit down with his sword as he was standing 5 tails away, Merrill used his Chi Force powers to grab the hapless rat by the throat. The rat struggled to breathe. Merrill then hoisted him up in the air and held him there for a moment before throwing him over the balcony rail. The rat fell to the factory floor below and landed with a thunderous crash causing all the workers to stop what they were doing. They all looked up in fear and stunned silence. Merrill walked over to the balcony rail to look down on his workers. "He failed in his mission. Because of that, we are now behind schedule." Merrill shouted. "The same fate awaits all of you if you do not make me a million coins and bars by the end of the week. Now clean up the mess and get back to work." Merrill ordered. He then muttered to himself, "I will have to send the Lemur Brothers to finish the candy store job."

Chapter Seven
The Lemur Brothers on Assignment

The Lemur Brothers are a notorious pair of mouse lemur twins, Wink and Voss. They have no particular allegiance to Goldmouse Sachs, Merrill Pynch or anyone else in the criminal underworld. They are instead up-and-coming crime bosses themselves who are willing to take work whenever they can to further their own interests. The twins have been dispatched by Merrill Pynch to do a job and have been given four rat soldiers to help them on their assignment. From their secret hideout in Smells Kitchen, the twins go over the plans for the heist with the four rats.

"Okay boys, here's what we're gonna do..." Wink began. "...we storm inside and take the girls by surprise. That way they won't have time to call for help or sound an alarm." Then Voss jumped in to finish his brother's thoughts as twins are often able to do.

"You two will restrain the girls." Voss said, pointing to two of the four rat soldiers. "If they give you any trouble, kill them! Number three, you will guard the door. And number four, you search the shop and take care of anyone else that might be in the store."

"Voss and I will clean out the shop," Wink said, finishing his brother's sentence. "We should be in and out in less than five minutes. Any questions?.. If not, let's move out and get to work."

The Lemur Brothers and their four rat soldiers head out from Smells Kitchen and make their way across town towards the United Candy Nations store. On their way, they encounter a dark tunnel which they must cross. As they enter the tunnel, they hear a hissing sound. In the shadows ahead they encounter three members of the infamous **Snake Syndicate**, George, Dickie and Blair. George is a Bushmaster snake. He is the gullible dumb one and the happy go-lucky member of the gang. Dickie the Death Adder is the ruthless cold-hearted snake of the Syndicate. He is second in command and the group's enforcer. Blair the Boa is the group's follower and cheerleader keen to make a name for himself. He thinks everything the Syndicate does is a great idea and eagerly jumps in to take part. The leader of the **SS** as they are sometimes called is a Chi Force sensitive spitting King Cobra named of **Madolf Hissler**. He is not with the Syndicate this day.

"Hello, my delicious victims. How nice to eat you." Dickie said snidely.

"Where are you going little brown rat? Come, have lunch with us in our underground flat." George laughed.

Dickie and his crew look to make an easy meal out of the Lemur Brothers and the rats. But the Lemur twins are feeling unusually brave against the Syndicate today. They tell the snakes, "You better get out of our way." The twins inform the snakes that they are on a mission for Goldmouse and that if they don't get out of the way, they will have to deal with Goldmouse. Madolf and Goldmouse are not friends, but they respect each other and sometimes join forces when it benefits them. Dickie, as ruthless and cold-hearted as he may be, doesn't dare to harm one of Goldmouse's underlings without Madolf's permission.

"Well, lucky for you we weren't that hungry anyways. We'll let you go this time." Dickie said. The snakes slithered aside and up against the walls of the tunnel to clear a path for the Lemurs and the rats to pass. The Lemur Brothers marched confidently and defiantly past the snakes. The rat soldiers that followed behind them were not so brave. They trembled with fear and their hands shook as they tightly clutched their weapons. Their legs wobbled with each guarded step they took as they walked tentatively past the snakes in a single line. When the last rat walked past the snakes, Dickie locked eyes with him. The last rat's little heart went racing. Dickie slowly opened his mouth to reveal his fangs. A small droplet of yellow liquid venom dripped from them. The rat was terrified but was unable to move. He was frozen with fear. Soon all the other rats in front also took notice. Suddenly, Dickie made a half lunging feint strike at them. All the rats instinctively jumped as they squealed in terror while they scurried away. Dickie, the cruel snake that he was, derived pleasure from other's misery. He laughed at the terrorized rats.

At the United Candy Nations store, Nadia and Diana are having an unusually slow day. They think it may be the result of the attempted robbery the other day. The girls are brainstorming ways to drum up business and get customers back in the store when a gang burst through the door. It was the Lemur Brothers and the rat soldiers. Two of the rats immediately jump over the counter to where the girls are standing. Nadia and Diana are each forcibly grabbed by a rat soldier and are thrown to the ground. The rats pinned the girls down each with their dirty feet and pointed their weapons at them. "**Don't move and don't make a sound!**" they ordered. Meanwhile, a third rat soldier ran around the store to make sure no one else was in the shop while the fourth guarded the front door. While that was happening, Wink and Voss quickly smashed the display cases and grabbed all the candy jewels they came for. Everything went just as the Lemurs planned and the gang was out in less than five minutes. Nadia and Diana couldn't believe what had just happened. It was so fast they didn't even have time to react. As soon as the gang left, they screamed for help. But by then, it was already too late. Diana quickly decided to call Soros and inform the Ninja Mice of the robbery.

The Ninja Mice came as quickly as they could. When they arrived, they found the candy store in shambles; broken glass and debris everywhere. Nadia and Diana were in tears. Soros and Buffy were the first to reach and tend to them. They hugged and comforted the girls while Knyse and René assessed the damage and looked for clues to what happened, who was responsible and why. The girls were shaken by the robbery but not physically harmed.

"There were six of them; four rats and a couple of mouse lemurs. They stormed in and did this!" Diana cried. "Our beautiful store is ruined. Those rats also threw us on to the ground and pinned us down with their dirty feet Now our beautiful clothes are ruined too."

"Well girls, the good news is that you two are only slightly hurt." said Soros. "What they stole from you can be replaced. We will help you clean up the store and make it good as new again. And as for your nice clothes... well, real beauty does not come from expensive clothes. It comes from the heart and how you love."

"Oh, that's a good one, Soros. I've got to write that down." said Knyse. His joke was meant to lighten the mood. He then teased, "Maybe you should kiss their **boo-boo** and make it better too."

Nadia did not take kindly to Knyse's joke. She stomped over to him with a mad frowny face and punched him in the arm. It was a friendly half punch, but a punch nonetheless. She followed that up by pinching and twisting his ear. Knyse sheepishly smiled as if to say, sorry.

Suddenly, Buffy detects a foul but familiar scent in the shop. He walks over to the girls to sample the air around them... **sniff-**

sniff, sniff-sniff... "Uh, girls... Did you two forget to shower this morning?" he asked as politely as he could.

"BUFFY!!!" the girls yell as they were mortified.

"It's a very faint but familiar odor. I think I actually like it." said Buffy. Everyone looked at him funny. "I think it's a Stenchbrick!" he continued. Buffy's super sensitive nose and love of food helped him to identify the smell. The others quickly realized he was right. It was the scent of a Stenchbrick. But where was it coming from? Everyone began to follow Buffy's nose.

"It must've been those jerks who robbed us!" said Diana. "Don't worry about helping us clean up here. Go find those creeps!"

Buffy and the rest of the Ninja Mice headed out. They followed the distinct scent trail down the street and through a series of tunnels. The mice later reach a junction where the scent trail split into two directions. In one direction, the scent trail leads to north of the city. The other and stronger scent trail leads to towards Smells Kitchen. "Well guys, looks like we're going back to Smells Kitchen." Knyse said. As the leader of the Ninja Mice, Knyse decided that it was best to stick together rather than split up and have two of them follow the second scent trail.

As the Ninja Mice reached Stinken Tunnel, the passage that leads in and out of Smells Kitchen, they immediately sensed danger. It was the Snake Syndicate. Dickie and his crew were still looking for their easy meal of the day. But he recognized the quartet as the Ninja Mice and realized they won't be the easy meal he was hoping for. "Hello ninjas!" said Dickie. "My, aren't you two plump and tasty looking." he said, referring to Soros and Buffy. "But not you two... You two are just skin and bones."

"Oh why thank you!" replied Buffy. "Yes, I do look plump but I am not tasty. I'm plump because I eat a lot of beans and so I'm gassy. Trust me; you don't want to eat me." Buffy joked.

"Ha! The truth finally comes out! It was you that farted at yoga last week." René yelled, thinking Buffy finally confessed.

"Hello snakes." Knyse greeted them with distain. "You must be Dickie, the Death Adder; the enforcer of the Snake Syndicate. We're not looking for any trouble. We're looking for a couple of mouse lemurs that robbed our friends' shop."

"Ha, you must be looking for the Lemur Brothers." George the Bushmaster snake shouted out excitedly. Dickie glared at George. He was not impressed with George giving away information like that. "We saw them this..."

"**Shut up, George!**" Dickie shouted; cutting George off before he could finish what he was saying. "As I was saying... we're hungry; you look tasty; let's eat. Get 'em boys!" Dickie ordered.

With that, Blair the Boa immediately lunged at Buffy with a strike that narrowly missed as Buffy jumped. George also lashed out. He tried to get both Knyse and René at the same time but ended up missing badly. The Ninja Mice used their Chi Force powers to anticipate and avoid George and Blair's attacks repeatedly.

Dickie, who waited for his opportunity to strike, then took aim at Soros. He salivated at the thought of making the big guy his meal. Dickie lunged viciously at him. But Soros was ready. As Dickie's jaws opened to its widest and ready to clamp down, Soros jammed his Bo Staff vertically into Dickie's mouth. Dickie's mouth was wedged open. He could not bite down nor open his mouth any further to get himself unstuck. Dickie was now as useless and harmless of a flailing garden hose with its water turned on full blast. He flopped wildly trying to dislodge Soros' Bo Staff.

Meanwhile, the fight turned into a 4-on-2 in favour of the Ninja Mice. And with the mice using their powers to avoid the snake strikes, George and Blair soon tired. The cold-blooded serpents did not have the **stamina** for a prolonged fight. The mice easily won this battle. But there was still the matter of retrieving Soros' Bo Staff from Dickie's mouth. That was taken care of by Buffy whacking Dickie over the head with his Nunchaku, knocking the snake unconscious. Soros was then able to safely take back his weapon. Once that was done, the mice continued on their way following the scent trail of the Stenchbrick. But unbeknownst to them, the commotion of their fight with the snakes attracted the attention of a recent **adversary**, the cigarette smoking Boss Rat. He watched the mice fight with the snakes from the shadows. Boss Rat had his right hand bandaged up from his encounter with René. He wanted revenge and so he decided to follow the mice to see where they were going and what they were up to.

The scent trail led the Ninja Mice to a small warehouse located at a dead end street at **1850 Cotton Avenue**. It was next to a set of railroad tracks that was seldom used. The building itself was nondescript and it lacked all but one window. The door of the warehouse was locked but the mice were able to peek through a dirty dusty window. From the outside, the mice looked in and saw the Lemur Brothers. They were alone and celebrating loudly.

"Our plan worked perfectly! We were in and out in no time all." the Lemur Brother said to each other proudly. "And did you see how scared those girls were?! Hahaha! That was so much fun, we should do it again."

Buffy was going to pick open the locked door so he and the rest of the Ninja Mice could sneak in quietly. But upon hearing the Lemur Brothers laugh at the expense of Nadia and Diana, the mice were mighty ticked off. Knyse and René were in rage mode by this point. Even happy-go-lucky Buffy was ready to punch someone in the face. Soros, wanting to get his hand on the lemurs right away, **SMASHED** the door open with a thunderous kick. The door flew off its hinges and scared the lemurs half to death. The Ninja Mice charged in at the lemurs and immediately surrounded them with their weapons drawn and ready to strike.

"So you think it's funny to rob and terrorize girls, huh?" Knyse sneered. And without any further warning, all four Ninja Mice attacked the lemurs; hitting them with their weapons and with kicks and punches. The lemurs were caught completely off guard and unable to defend themselves. Soros punched and elbowed one of the lemurs. René kicked the other in the face with a **tail-kwon-do spinning roundhouse**. The lemurs were battered and beaten senseless. Knyse grabbed one of the brothers and yelled, "Where are the candies you stole?!! Where?! Answer me!"

Wink: "We don't have them. We don't have them."

Knyse: "Then where are they? What did you do with them?"

Voss: "The rats have them. We gave them to the rats to take back to their master. We were only hired to do the job."

Knyse: "Who hired you? What do they want with the candies?"

Wink: "Merrill Pynch hired us. He's called Number Two. He just told us to steal the candies. We don't know what they're planning to do with it. He and his master just wanted them and we didn't ask."

Knyse: "So this Merrill Pynch character is real, huh. Who does #2
work for? Who is #2's master?"

But before either one of the brothers could answer, a loud
rumble interrupted the interrogation. The rumble grew louder
and closer with every passing moment. Then a familiar train horn
blast was heard. It was a freight train and it sounded like it was
headed right at them. The warehouse began to tremble as the
train got closer and closer. As it passed, the entire building shook.
The tremors settled only after the train cleared the area.

Everyone breathed a sigh of relief when everything returned to
normal. But then everyone heard a **THUD** and a dull **BOOM**,
followed by another; then another; and another... It was coming
from a nearby closet. The door of the closet began to bulge and
buckle. The terrified lemurs ran to the door as quickly as they
could. Both Wink and Voss pushed back against the bulging
closet door with their shoulders to prevent whatever was inside
from collapsing. But the pressure behind the door was mounting.
The twins pushed back hard as they dug in their heels. But their
feet were slipping. The door hinges began to buckle under the
strain. The momentum soon became too great for the brothers
to hold back. The door suddenly burst open and the contents
that were being held back began to tumble and cascade down on
to Wink and Voss. At the same time, noxious fumes poured out
from the closet. What fell out was the biggest load of Stenchbrick

blue cheese anyone had ever seen. There must have been over 10,000 wheels of the toxic stuff all of which were the **Subprime** version. The entire inventory of unstable stacks of cheese just collapsed on the Lemur Brothers; crushing them. The Ninja Mice were in shock and awe. They were overjoyed by the sight of all the delicious blue cheese. They realized then that all the missing Stenchbrick from New Mouse City had been stolen and hoarded by the Lemur Brothers. Soon a fog of toxic fumes began to fill the warehouse. The mice held their breath and waded through the cloud to find the lemurs. The twins were pinned underneath a mountain of rubble and dying.

"Who does #2 work for?" **Cough-Cough** "Who is #2's master?" **Cough-Cough** "Who's behind all this?" **Cough-Cough**... Knyse struggled to breathe and ask questions. All the mice had trouble breathing. They coughed uncontrollably and started to feel light headed. Their eyes watered and their noses burned. The lemurs were incoherent as they began to hallucinate. They rambled on about how they loved #2 first thing in the morning and that golden mice are scary. What the heck were they talking about, the mice wondered. As the Lemur Brothers were still trapped under the pile of Subprime Stenchbrick dying, the Ninja Mice had no choice but to leave them behind. The mice risked permanent brain damage if they stayed and tried to rescue the lemurs.

Chapter Eight
Merrill Pynch Robs a Bank

It's another busy day at the basement level of the old chocolate factory. Merrill Pynch is once again on a video conference call with Goldmouse Sachs. Merrill tells Goldmouse that the Lemur Brothers were successful and that the rats had returned with the candy jewels. With the fake jewels in hand, the counterfeit money printed and almost a million chocolate gold coins bars, they are ready to proceed with their plans to rob banks. When Merrill finished his call, there was a knock on his door. It was Boss Rat from Smells Kitchen. Although he is physically bigger than Merrill Pynch, Boss Rat knows that size does not always matter. More importantly, he knows Pynch's reputation for being ruthless and unforgiving. Boss Rat is standing outside Merrill's office looking very nervous clutching his bandaged and broken hand. Merrill, using his Chi Force powers, sensed both Boss Rat's nervousness and that he had something important to tell him.

"Master Pynch, sir… **mmmmy** name is Killer Karl the Rat, but you can just call me **KKR**. I'm the boss of the **Nabisco** Gang. I saw the Ninja Mice in Smells Kitchen yesterday. I was alone and I followed them." Boss Rat told Pynch. He went on to tell Merrill that he followed the mice to the Lemur Brothers' warehouse. There he saw the lemur twins confess to robbing the United Candy Nations store while implicating him and Goldmouse. Merrill Pynch was not happy to hear this. He now knows the Ninja Mice know about him and Goldmouse and that they are up to something big. Merrill was so upset that Boss Rat feared he might end up on the receiving end of Pynch's wrath. But Boss Rat had some good news for Merrill. He reported that the twins were later crushed to death by an avalanche of toxic Stenchbricks that they had been hoarding. Afterwards, Boss Rat said he followed the Ninja Mice back to the candy store where he saw them help the owners, Nadia and Diana, clean up the mess from the robbery. When that was done, he said he followed the mice home and learned the secret location of their dojo. Upon hearing this, Merrill Pynch was extremely pleased.

"Excellent work!" Merrill shouted at Boss Rat who was trembling the whole time. "And for your fine work, I will reward you by making you one of my lieutenants. From now on, anyone who dares to cross you will have to answer to me! Now come, let me fix your broken hand." Merrill placed his hands on Boss Rat's bandaged paw. He used his Chi Force Energy to accelerate the healing of Boss Rat's broken bones. "Your hand will be good as new in a couple of days." said Merrill. He then ordered Boss Rat to leave the chocolate factory and go back to Smells Kitchen. Boss Rat thanked Merrill Pynch for his kindness and wondered if Merrill was really the ruthless tyrant everyone thinks he is.

After Boss Rat left, Merrill Pynch assembled his entire rat army on the factory floor. He addressed them from the balcony of his office. "We are ready to proceed to the next phase of our plan." Merrill announced. "Tonight, I will take 500 of you with me to the surface world. There we will empty the vaults of Citibank. Soon we'll have so much money and wealth that no one can stop us."

Meanwhile, back at the dojo, the Ninja Mice have informed Grandmaster Greenspan about the Lemur Brothers' confession. Because the twins were **delirious** and **incoherent** towards the end, they can only speculate on the meaning of "golden mice are scary." Greenspan and the mice are very concerned that it may be a reference to Goldmouse Sachs. And if that's the case, then Goldmouse is still alive. Could that also mean Merrill Pynch is working for Goldmouse and that's why he is referred to as #2 they wondered. If so, then there must be a big sinister plan in the works. To confirm their suspicion and what that plan might be, Greenspan instructs the mice to scour the city and find the truth.

That evening, Merrill Pynch and his army of 500 rat soldiers surfaced from the basement level of the chocolate factory to the ground floor in uptown New York. It is late November and the sky is dark. The night is cold like Merrill Pynch's heart. The air bites shrewdly; winter is coming. Merrill's army is organized into 5 teams. Each team consisting of 100 rats is led by a General and seconded by a Major. Merrill and his Generals and Majors each ride in their own battery powered modified Lego Technic vehicles using Power Functions while the rest march alongside. The entire army is jubilant believing it will be a triumphant night. The army convoy make their way from uptown New York through Central Park. They march their way towards midtown with stealth and bad intentions. Along the way, the rat soldiers march and chant:

```
              ┌──────────┐
              │ General  │
              └────┬─────┘
              ┌────┴─────┐
              │  Major   │
              └────┬─────┘
         ┌─────────┴─────────┐
    ┌────┴────┐         ┌────┴────┐
    │ Captain │         │ Captain │
    └────┬────┘         └────┬────┘
    ┌────┴────┐         ┌────┴────┐
┌───────────┐ ┌───────────┐ ┌───────────┐ ┌───────────┐
│2 Lieutenant│ │2 Lieutenant│ │2 Lieutenant│ │2 Lieutenant│
│22 Rat Soldiers│ │22 Rat Soldiers│ │22 Rat Soldiers│ │22 Rat Soldiers│
└───────────┘ └───────────┘ └───────────┘ └───────────┘
```

I don't know what I've been told
I don't know what I've been told
Rats are worth their weight in gold
Rats are worth their weight in gold
And penguin butts are mighty cold
And penguin butts are mighty cold
Do they use a toilet bowl?
Do they use a toilet bowl?
No they don't, they dig a hole
No they don't, they dig a hole
Then they drop their lump of coal
Then they drop their lump of coal
Where they do their business, I don't care
Where they do their business, I don't care
Just as long as they don't share
Just as long as they don't share
Sound-off: 1 - 2
Sound-off: 3 - 4
1 - 2 - 3 - 4
1 - 2 …… 3 - 4

The convoy arrive at its destination, Citibank, in the late hours at night. The streets are all empty and there's no one around except a lone security guard inside the bank. The guard is a young man in a blue uniform.

His duty is to protect the premises and physical belongings of the bank from would be thieves and vandals. The bank's valuables such as paper money, gems and jewels are kept inside a vault. Most gems and jewels belong to the customers of the bank and are stored in safety deposit boxes which are located inside the vault. Aside from the guard on duty, the bank is also protected by an **elaborate alarm system**. Along with it, there are security cameras everywhere, motion sensors that activate the alarm and smoke detectors and sprinklers for fires. The vault itself is made of thick solid steel and the walls of the bank are made of reinforced concrete that can withstand a bomb blast or an earthquake; not that you would ever get an earthquake in New York. Part of the security guard's job is to routinely walk around the bank to check on noises, look for anything unusual, make sure all the doors are locked and to make sure everything is working fine. He does his walkabout once an hour, every hour.

When Merrill and his troops arrive at the front entrance of the bank, they find the guard at his desk monitoring the security cameras. He appears bored and inattentive. It's understandable considering most of the time nothing ever happens so his job can be quite boring. The most excitement he gets on a typical night might be to shoo away a drunken reveler urinating against the side of the building on his way home from a late night out at the bars. Merrill decides to take his troops to the back of the bank where they can enter from the alley.

The back of the bank is a narrow alley way with a dumpster. The building is a flat brick wall with a solid windowless metal door and a small air vent. Merrill could have used his Chi Force powers to easily rip the door open, but that would have triggered the bank's alarm. So instead, he took a small team of 12, a lieutenant and 11 soldiers, to crawl through the air ventilation. The air vent was just big enough for them to fit. Once inside, the rats had to be very careful not to accidentally set off the alarm system. Merrill directed his troops to locate the electrical panel and fuse box to deactivate the bank's security systems while he deals with the guard.

Merrill and his troops could have easily overpowered the guard and tied him up or even killed him if they wanted. With his powers and the sheer number of rat soldiers at his command, that would have been very easy. But Merrill's goal was to rob the bank unnoticed. Confronting the guard would have undermined that goal. From the air vent high above in the ceiling, Merrill planned his attack. He stared intently at the guard below. Merrill was filled with rage and hatred. He did not know the guard personally, but he wanted to kill him badly nonetheless. Merrill despised humans and the guard just happened to be in his way. Merrill hates all humans because blames them for the death of his family. So to him, all humans deserve to die. Merrill wasn't always an evil ruthless killer. He was once an ordinary hard working lad with a corporate job, a wife and three young children. Back then, he was just another employee in the **corporate rat race** working as a research analyst for the investment bank **Morgan Squeaky**. Merrill left the corporate world when his family died in an accident at the hands of a human. Goldmouse Sachs discovered him shortly after that. The death of his family is the source of much of Merrill's hate and anger.

From the air vent, Merrill quietly descends to the floor to sneak up behind the guard. The guard is sitting in his chair watching the camera monitor and enjoying a hot cup of cocoa; a fitting beverage for the season. Merrill hides behind the guard's chair before sneaking over to the desk. From the floor, he stealthily climbed up the side of the desk to hide behind the guard's cup of cocoa. There, Merrill quickly drops a sleeping pill into the guard's drink. Afterwards, he climbs back down to the floor and returns to the air vent to wait for the drug to take effect.

While Merrill dealt with the security guard, his troops located the bank's electrical panel and fuse box. They **franticly chewed** on the wires that powered the security cameras, motion sensors and alarm system. By the time the rats chewed through the wires, the guard was fast asleep. It was now safe to move about freely inside the bank. Merrill's lieutenant then went to open the bank's back door to let in the rest of the army. Hundreds of excited rats poured into the bank like a mini flood. They could not wait to get to work.

Merrill's Rat Generals and Majors unloaded power tools from their vehicles. The tools they had included power drills, screw drivers, hammers, wrenches, pliers and lock picking gadgets. The rat soldiers eagerly began to dismantle and unlock the vault. They were **calm and deliberate** in their task. There was no need to rush as the guard was asleep and the bank's security system was disabled. Once the vault and the safety deposit boxes were picked open, the rats carried out all the valuables. They emptied millions of dollars worth of diamonds, rubies, emeralds and whatever else they could find. They then carefully replaced all the real gems and jewelry with fakes they stole from the United Candy Nations store. The rats also took hundreds of millions of dollars in cash and replaced it with the counterfeit money they printed.

When the rats were done, they carefully re-assembled and locked up the vault. Before leaving, the rats also reattached the wires they chewed through by using black electrical tape. The whole bank robbery from beginning to end took about 5 hours to complete. Because of his careful and deliberate planning, Merrill was confident the theft would go undiscovered for many days or even weeks. By then, Merrill will have had a chance to rob many more banks before anyone notices the fake gems and counterfeit money; a brilliant masterplan hatched up by the evil genius, Goldmouse Sachs.

From the alley behind the bank, Merrill and his troops head underground and make their way northward with hundreds of millions in cash and jewels in tow. Rather than take the same route back to the factory, Merrill decided it was best to use the tunnels and sewers of New Mouse City. Even though it was 4:00 AM in the morning, there was still a chance Merrill and his troops could be spotted by someone if they used a surface route home. As they made their way through various tunnels, the rats once again march and chant: **I don't know what I've been told.** The rats all marched and chanted loudly and fearlessly. As a group, they felt untouchable; strong and invincible. They were afraid of nothing and no one.

As a smart military commander, Merrill sent a small team to walk 500 tails ahead of the rest of the convoy. The tactical scout team was made up of 1 Captain and 2 Lieutenants. Their job was to walk far in front to look out for potential obstacles and dangers for the rest of the group. The scout team was quick and nimble. In order to make it in the rat army, one has to be cunning and courageous. And to move up the ranks, you have to be willing to do anything and take chances to prove yourself worthy. The trio in the scout team were especially brave and ambitious. The rank of Lieutenant was Merrill Pynch's rank when he first joined Goldmouse's rat army.

As the scout team led the convoy through New Mouse City, all was quiet and normal in the tunnels. They were half way home to the factory and it seemed as the journey would be uneventful. But then suddenly up ahead the trio heard a hissing sound. Out of the shadows, three vicious looking snakes appear. It was the Snake Syndicate gang; George, Dickie and Blair. The trio of rats stop dead in their tracks. The snakes smiled gleefully. Dickie and Blair flicked their tongues out to taste the air while George licked his chops. "Hello, my delicious furry friends. What brings you out so late at night?" Dickie asked rhetorically.

The rats didn't know what to say or do. They just stood there with their eyes locked on the snakes. Adrenaline and a sense of panic rushed through their little bodies; their heart rate spiking. Should they run or should they stand and fight the rats thought to themselves. Fighting the snakes didn't seem like a smart idea. The rats were brave little soldiers, but not that brave. Nor were they that stupid either. As the snakes prepared to strike, their attention was distracted by the sounds of stomping and chanting. They heard a chorus of "..**Penguin butts are mighty cold.**" It was the rest of the rat army convey. As the rest of the group caught up with the scout team and came into view of the snakes, Dickie realized his small easy meal just became a big problem that he wasn't going to be able to swallow. George on the other hand thought his easy meal just turned into a massive all you can eat buffet. George couldn't wait any longer. He wasted no time in launching his strike at the rats. George recklessly flung himself forward fang first with a lunging jab. His mouth was wide open ready to clamp down as soon as his lips touched a rat. But what he got instead was a brick in his face. **WHAM!** It was Merrill Pynch using his Chi Force to throw a brick at George.

Dazed and confused, George was left seeing stars. He picked himself up, gathered his sense and readied himself for another strike. As George lunged forward, he was met with an invisible force that grabbed him by the throat choking him. **ACKK-CUH-KAHK-ARGH-ACKK.** George struggled to breathe as he was being choked out. Dickie and Blair were alarmed and puzzled to understand what was happening to George. Then the sea of rats parted and Merrill Pynch waded through the crowd, his hand held up to mimic a strangling motion. It was clear to Dickie at that moment what was happening and who was choking George. Although this was the first time Dickie and Merrill encountered each other, they both knew each other by reputation. Blair on the other hand was a little bit more clueless. He sort of knows who Merrill was, but was more eager to join the fight than use reason. Blair was poised to strike at Merrill but Dickie held him back. "Let him go, Merrill or you'll have to deal with the entire Syndicate gang." Dickie firmly ordered.

Merrill releases his choke hold on George who immediately collapses to the ground. "So, you must be Dickie. Madolf Hissler's number two in command, huh?"

Knowing they were greatly outnumbered, Dickie, put on a brave face to say, "And you must be the great big bad Merrill Pynch; Goldmouse's number two... We're not interested in a fight with you, but we'll give you one if you want it. We could use an easy meal you know."

"No, an eye for an eye will leave the world blind. So a fight, just for the sake of a fight will not benefit either one of us. But I do have an offer that might. It's a proposition from Goldmouse for you to take back to Madolf. Tell Madolf to get in touch with us."

Dickie didn't want to appear weak and back down; especially to a rat. But Merrill's words gave Dickie and his crew a way out and to save face. As the two sides parted ways, Dickie was very intrigued by what Goldmouse might have in mind. He was eager to return to base and relay the message to his master, Madolf Hissler.

Chapter Nine
All is Not Right in the Banking World

It's been over two weeks since Merrill Pynch robbed Citibank. In that time, the Ninja Mice have scoured the city for clues to confirm if Goldmouse is still alive, what he is up to, where he might be hiding and whether or not Merrill Pynch works for him. So far, the mice have not had a lot of luck. They are back at their dojo doing their daily training and exercises and thinking about their next move. The mice are in the dungeon room taking turns to do the obstacle course when Grandmaster Greenspan strolled in with a newspaper in his hand.

"Ninjas, stop what thou art doing and cometh here now." said Grandmaster. He tells his Ninja Mice about an article he read in the newspaper. The article talks about a woman who tried to withdraw money from her bank account at a bank machine but was unable. Every machine she went to she got the same message: *'This machine is temporarily out of cash.'* The article went on to say that the woman had to go into the bank in person to takeout money from her account. And when she did, she discovered her bank closes early these days. Not only that, she also learned the amount of money she could withdraw was capped at $100 a day. Grandmaster went on to tell the mice that he has read similar articles in the last few days involving other people and other banks. "Ninja, I sense a great disturbance in the

Chi Force. There is an extraordinary level of anxiety and panic amongst the people around us. Ye shall go investigate at once."

Meanwhile over at the chocolate factory, Goldmouse Sachs has arrived with his pilot and assistant, **Tina Tereshkova**. They are with Merrill Pynch and together they are celebrating in a room filled with billions in cash and jewels. Goldmouse is downright gleeful and giddy as he cuddles the stacks of money. Over the last two weeks, Merrill and the troops have robbed many more banks leaving the city virtually cashless.

"Merrill, you have done well." Goldmouse said proudly. "I can feel the fear amongst the surface dwellers. Their police must be on high alert by now. But tonight, we will still launch our final strike as planned. We will bring their economy and financial system to their knees, **MUHAHA!** Merrill, help Tina to load **$10 million dollars** into her airplane for tonight."

As Goldmouse gave his instructions to Merrill Pynch and Tina, they heard a noise from outside the room. Goldmouse sensed an uninvited intruder outside their locked room. Using his Chi Force power, he opened the door to reveal it was Boss Rat who was eavesdropping on their conversation. "Who are you and how daringly dumb of you to spy on us?" Goldmouse asked.

Boss Rat trembled with so much fear for being caught that he nearly soiled his underpants. Unable to speak, Merrill chimed in to speak for him, "That is Killer Karl the Rat, Master. I told you about him. He is the ore that followed the Ninja Mice and discovered the secret location of their dojo. I made him one my lieutenants."

"I'm sorry ssssir. I didn't mean to eavesdrop. I only came to check in with Master Merrill like he asked to every couple of weeks. I was told he was here in this room but I didn't know if should interrupt when I overheard your conversation. I'm very sorry."

Goldmouse was not happy with the intruder. But at the same time, he was happy with the information he provided. "Merrill, he heard our plans for tonight. Because of this, you must take him with you tonight and make sure he does not betray us."

While that was happening at the factory, the Ninja Mice surfaced to New York City to speak to their friend and reporter, **Walter Leland**. Walter is a highly respected investigative journalist who works for the EBS Evening News. They met with their other friend, Jeremy, for lunch at his restaurant, Jeremy the Jerk.

"Walter," Knyse said, "there are stories in the newspaper about bank machines being out of money and in-person withdrawals at banks are capped at $100 a day. Grandmaster Greenspan is very concerned because he senses a lot of fear and concern. What's going on, Walter?"

"Yeah Walter, I'd like to know too." Jeremy added. "I deposited $5000 in my bank last week from my restaurant business. I tried to take some money out the other day and I was told I could only take out $100. When I spoke with the bank manager, he told me they were temporarily low on cash. His explanation was that the armored vehicle that fills all the bank machines and drops off cash to the bank branches from the head office didn't make its delivery to his bank. I said to him that was outrageous! I have vendors to pay and supplies to buy to run my business. **How can I operate with just $100?!**"

"What's in the newspaper is just the tip of the iceberg." said Walter. "I've done some digging and have discovered something very bad. The reason why the armored trucks aren't making their deliveries is there is no money to deliver. I've been told by my sources inside the banks that they've all been robbed."

Jeremy and the Ninja Mice are shocked to learn the truth. "What do you mean – *all the banks*? Who's been robbed?" asked Knyse.

"I mean **ALL** of them." Walter replied. "Every major bank in town has been robbed! The banks themselves don't know this yet, but I know because I talked to the heads of all the different banks. They all told me the same thing; they didn't even realize they were robbed until some customers complained about the cash they were given. When their customers complained, the bank realized the cash they were giving out was counterfeit. When they checked their vault, they realized all the bills they had were all fake. Their vault and all contents of their safety deposit boxes had been robbed and replaced with fakes; all done without a trace. Police and officials are investigating, but so far nobody knows how or who did it. There's very little evidence except for the fake money and candy jewels left behind. This city is almost completely out of cash and the bank managers that I've talked to are scared to death. They're in full panic mode and don't know what to do."

"That's awful, Walter!" Knyse said. "Why haven't you reported this to the public? People have the right to know and you should tell them. They trust you... And wait, did you say candy jewels?"

Walter then pulled out a picture of the candy jewels taken from the crime scene. He shows it to the Ninja Mice who immediately recognize it as the missing candies from Nadia and Diana's store. They knew then it was Merrill Pynch who was behind the bank robberies. That also meant Goldmouse Sachs was likely still alive and **orchestrating** the whole thing.

"It's a bit of a dilemma." said Walter. "You're right Knyse; people do have the right to know. And it is my job as a journalist to tell the truth. But if I do so now, it would only create public panic and a run on the banks. That is not in the public's interest as it would only create more problems... maybe even chaos and riots."

"**A run on the banks?** What does that mean? And why would people riot?" the Ninja Mice all asked.

Jeremy was horrified. "I'll tell you what it mean." he said. "It means people like me who deposited $5000 in the bank are the only reason they are still open. If the public knew the truth, then everyone would rush to their bank to get their money out. In the case of my bank, it would only take 50 people to withdraw $100 each before it runs out of money; this would lead to more panic as everyone will demand to have all their money back. And when they can't get it, there will be riots!"

The mice were all shocked as they realized the magnitude of the problem at hand. Jeremy went on to explain to them about the banking system and how it works. For example, he said, if you put $100 in the bank, the bank does not keep your $100 in its vault. It only keeps about $10 and lends out $90 to other people who need to borrow money to buy a house or start a business. The $90 that is spent by the borrower will eventually come back to the bank as a deposit by another person. And of that $90 deposit, only about $9 is kept by the bank and $81 is lent out to new borrowers. This process continues on and on until there is no more money the bank can lend out.

Your original $100 is the amount of money initially circulating in the economy. By depositing your cash into the bank, the bank was able to lend money out and create new deposits. Eventually, the amount of money it w ll able to lend out is $900. At the same time, the bank owes $1000 in customer deposits while having only $100 in actual cash in their vault to give back to their customers.

The reason you put your money in the bank is because it is a safe place to keep it. And the bank pays you interest too. That means they pay you money for your deposit. The reason the bank does not keep all the money you deposited in its vault is because they have to make a profit to pay for the interest they owe you for your deposit. And the bank also believes you will not withdraw all the money you deposited all at once. Of the $100 you deposited, they believe you might take out $5 or $6 at a time. It may stay in your pocket or wallet for a period of time but the bank believes it will eventually come back to the banking system as a deposit. Generally, the bank believes $10 or 10% is the most you will ever really takeout. So this is the amount they keep in their vault. The rest they lend out to make a profit. This is called fractional reserve banking and it is how banks are able to increase the amount of money available to people and circulating in the economy. This increase is called the multiplier effect. The 10% is the reserve ratio.

In terms of interest, let's say the bank pays you $0.40 for the $100 you deposited. Because the bank has created $1000 in total deposits due to lending and redeposits, they will have to pay a total of $4.00 in interest to depositors. Now let's say the bank charges $7.00 on every $100 they lend out. Because they lent out a total of $900, the bank can expect to receive $63 in interest from their borrowers. From this, they will be able to pay their depositors the interest they promised. The left amount (63-4=59) is the profit the bank keeps. Starting with only the original $100, the bank was able to make a $59 profit… not bad, huh! The difference in interest the bank pays depositors (0.40) and what it charges borrowers (7.00) is called the ***interest rate spread*** (6.60).

"So now that you understand the **banking system**, here's the problem," Jeremy added. "If $100 represents all the reserve money that was stolen from all the banks, then the size of the problem and the impact to everyone is $1000. But that's only if we assumed the reserve ratio is 10%. What if the banks kept a lot less than 10% and lent out a lot more in loans? If they only kept, say, 5% in reserve, then the financial impact will be $2000 on $100 of stolen reserve money. Based on what Walter just told us, a heck of a lot more than $100 was stolen. Maybe billions! Our economy and financial system could collapse like a house of cards. People may have to switch back to using gold for a while! I hope the gold is still safe at the New York Federal Reserve Bank."

The Ninja Mice were stunned and fascinated to learn all this from Jeremy. Then it suddenly dawned on Knyse. "I know who behind all this and what his next target is." Knyse cried. "It's Goldmouse! He's alive and he has a new apprentice, Merrill Pynch! Their next target is the Federal Reserve Bank. And I'll bet you it's going down tonight!"

Walter and Jeremy were horrified by Knyse's revelation. They remember what the city and everyone had to endure the last time Goldmouse attacked. "How are you so sure he's going after the Federal Reserve Bank? And why tonight?" They both asked.

"We know it's Goldmouse because he loves gold. **And the Federal Reserve Bank has the largest deposit of gold in the world**. So it makes perfect sense for him to go after it." Knyse explained. "It's going to happen tonight because there's a full moon tonight! This is when Goldmouse and Merrill will be at their most powerful. We have to go now before it's too late!

Chapter Nine
Bonus Extra

The Federal Reserve Bank of New York is located near Wall Street. The Bank maintains a vault at its basement floor that lies 80 feet (24 meters) below street level and into New Mouse City resting on solid bedrock. By 1927, the vault contained 10% of the world's official gold reserves. Much of the gold in the vault arrived during and after World War II as many countries wanted to store their gold reserves in a safe location. Currently, it is reputedly the largest gold repository in the world (this cannot be confirmed as Swiss banks do not report their gold stocks). At its peak, the vault contained over 12,000 tonnes (nearly 400 million ounces) of gold bullion worth hundreds of billions of dollars. Nearly 98% of the gold at the Bank is owned by the central banks of foreign countries. The rest is owned by the United States and international organizations such as the International Monetary Fund (IMF). The Federal Reserve Bank does not own the gold but serves as guardian of the precious metal, which it stores at no charge to the owners.

Chapter Ten
The Biggest Gold Heist Ever

After meeting with Walter and Jeremy, the Ninja Mice rushed over to the Federal Reserve Bank of New York. They arrived in the late afternoon while the Bank was still open but it was near the end of the business day. The mice had to figure out a way to get inside without being seen or caught. They needed to get down to the vault in the basement to see if the gold was still there safe and sound. But the bank was well protected by armed security guards. As luck would have it, the Ninja Mice arrived on a day when the Bank was having a tour for a group of school children. They came just as the tour began. The mice saw their opportunity when the last child of the group, a little girl, was about to go through security check. Unbeknownst to the mice, the little girl in line was the same child who met Greenspan on the airplane a few weeks ago. The little girl walked through the metal detector as her backpack passed through the x-ray machine. When her backpack cleared, the Ninja Mice jumped inside the backpack. The little girl picked up her backpack and rejoined her group. The school children then rode the elevator down to the gold vault in the basement.

Inside the backpack, the Ninja Mice were enjoying themselves. Especially Buffy as he found the little girl's lunch box. **sniff-sniff** "Hey guys, look what I found. Cheese sticks!!!" Buffy proclaimed excitedly. "Blueberries and grapes, too! Yum! **Fruits are mother nature's candy**. And crackers! This is the best field trip ever!"

"Buffy! Put that back." Knyse yelled. "That's her lunch. You can't eat that. She'll go hungry if you do."

"But... but..." Buffy sighed as he tried to come up with an excuse or reason that would allow him to get away with eating the little girl's lunch. "...it's so delicious." Buffy whimpered reluctantly. He knew it was not the right thing to do. "Oh look, she's got ketchup packs here too. Can I at least eat this?" Buffy asked sarcastically.

"Guys, we're here!" said Soros. He was peeking out the backpack. "I can see the gold. Come take a look!" The other mice all rush over and jockey for a view. "Wow! Look at all that gold. So this is what the largest deposit of gold in the world looks like, huh?! Do you think it's all real?"

"There's only one way to find out for sure." said Knyse. "René, since you're the quickest and most stealthy, you go and touch it and make sure it's real."

The tour group and the Ninja Mice are in the basement near the vault area. They can see the gold from a distant but are not allowed to go anywhere near it. Inside the vault, there are 122 compartments where the gold is stored. The compartments are a series of connected cages that resemble jail cells enclosed by steel bars. Each compartment and the gold inside is owned by an account holder such as a foreign country or government. René, being quick and tiny, was able to dash over to the compartments without being seen. He was able to touch the gold. And when he did, he knew they were real. Afterwards, René ran back to rejoin the others inside the little girl's backpack.

"Yep, they're real… and HEAVY!" said René. "If Goldmouse and Merrill are planning to rob this place, how the heck are they going to move all this gold? There's just so much!"

"That's a great question." replied Knyse. "Right now, I have no idea. But I just know they're going to hit this place tonight."

The tour in the basement did not last long. Soon the group was back up on the main floor of the bank in the museum section to learn about the history of the Bank. As the tour of the Bank was winding down, the mice knew they would be leaving soon. They would need to leave with the tour group or be locked inside the Bank when it closed. The mice realized that being locked inside would not be the best idea. Any move they make after hours could trigger the alarm system. And what if they were wrong? What if Goldmouse and Merrill aren't planning to rob the Bank? Or they are; but just not tonight? The mice would be locked in all night until the next day. There were too many scenarios to think about. Then Knyse came up with a great idea.

"Guys, I have a great idea." said Knyse. "Buffy, grab the cheese sticks from the little girl's lunch box. And René, give me your laxatives. I know you always have some ready to use on someone as a prank. We're going to use the laxatives and the cheese sticks to set a trap for the rats if they strike here tonight."

"**Oh, that is soooo nasty and evil of you**." René said gleefully as he knew and approved of what Knyse was thinking.

The Ninja Mice worked quickly to mix the laxatives into the cheese sticks. They then snuck out of the little girl's backpack they had been riding in during the tour. The mice went over to the elevator where they found nooks and **crevasses** to lay their trap. As they were doing so, something caught René's eyes. "Guys, I have to use the washroom." said René. "Finish without me and I'll meet you back at the backpack."

René was not being entirely honest with his friends. He saw a roll of clear scotch tape at the security guard's desk and realized there was an opportunity to pull off an epic prank. After he grabbed the tape, René ran back to the little girl's backpack to grab the ketchup packets from her lunch box. From there, René ran to the washroom where he found 4 toilet stalls. He quickly went to work taping the ketchup packs under all the toilet seats. Afterwards, he taped the toilet lids down tightly. Lastly, René wrapped tape all around the toilet paper. Because scotch tape is clear, the victim of René's prank would see there is paper in the stall, but they would not realize it would be next to impossible to dispense and use the paper until it was too late. When he finished setting up his prank, René met everyone back at the backpack. Soon thereafter, the tour was over and the group left the Bank which closed shortly after. The mice also snuck out the little girl's backpack and parted ways with the group. The mice then decided to stake out the Bank and watch for the rats from the roof of an adjacent building.

As evening approached at the chocolate factory, Goldmouse and Merrill marshaled their rat soldiers and prepared to head out. Goldmouse's pilot, Tina Tereshkova, readies her airplane that had been loaded with **$10 million in cash**. She has been instructed by Goldmouse to initiate her part of the plan for tonight at exactly 9 PM. As the sun sets, a full moon begins to appear in the evening sky. Goldmouse and Merrill both feel a surge of Chi Force energy flow through them Although a full moon allows them to grow in physical size, this effect caused by the **planetary alignment** can be controlled. Goldmouse and Merrill chose not to use the Chi Growth effect for now as they and their rat soldiers headed out towards the Federal Reserve Bank. They believed that by staying in their smaller form, they would remain better concealed and go unnoticed as they break into the Bank.

As early evening turned into late night, the Ninja Mice patiently waited at the Federal Reserve Bank. They had been there for hours watching and waiting for any sign that Goldmouse Sachs or

Merrill Pynch might be trying to rob the Bank. But they are growing restless as nothing has happened. The appearance of the full moon has also affected the mice. But they have also decided not to use the Chi Growth effect to transform into larger size. They pass the time on the roof of the building adjacent to the Bank by telling jokes to one another.

Soros: "Knock, knock."
Buffy: "Who's there?"
Soros: "Spell."
Buffy: "Spell who?"
Soros: "W-H-O"

René: "What's a cat's favourite breakfast?"
Soros: "I don't know. What?"
René: "Mice Crispy!"
Buffy: "That's a terrible joke."

Buffy: "Okay guys, I have a confession to make. It was me that farted in yoga class that time."
René: "Ah-ha! I knew it! I knew it!!!"
Buffy: "Not only that, my family is also predisposed to diarrhea. It runs in our jeans"
René: "Doh! Arrrggghhh!!!"

Knyse: "There are two kinds of mice in the world. The first kind can deal with incomplete information."

René: "And the second? What's the second kind??... Doh!"
Soros: "Yeah, what is the second kind??... Doh!"

René: "Why did the chicken cross the playground?"
Soros: "Why?"
René: "To get to the other slide!"
Knyse: "Oh brother... I dream one day to living in a kinder; more just world... One where chickens can cross the road and not have their motives questioned."

Meanwhile in the tunnels directly under the Federal Reserve Bank, Goldmouse, Merrill and their troops have arrived. They used an underground route through New Mouse City to reach the Bank rather than a surface one. There is a general heightened state of alert within the law enforcement community in New York due to all the recent bank robberies. Goldmouse was wise to use subsurface route to avoid detection. But from the tunnel below, there is no direct passage or connection into the underground vault of the Bank. The vault is completely self-contained and the only way in or out is by using the elevator from the main floor of the Bank on the ground level. Fortunately for the rats, they are able to reach the main floor lobby of the bank from their tunnel location. As with all the previous bank robberies, Merrill leads a small team 12 to first neutralize the Bank's security system and guard. But this time, Killer Karl the Rat (Boss Rat of the Nabisco gang) is with them too, so that makes it Merrill plus a team of 13. Goldmouse and the rest of the troops wait down below in the tunnels while Merrill and his team surfaced to the lobby where they must wait. The main entrance lobby doors into the Bank were locked. Merrill could easily break in by himself but he has been told to wait for Tina Tereshkova to make her move at 9 PM.

Elsewhere in the sky above midtown New York, Tina Tereshkova is circling in her airplane loaded with $10 million in cash. In recent days, the people of New York have become wary and concerned about their banks. They have become increasingly distressed by the lack of money they have and able to take out of their bank account. At exactly 9 PM, Tina began to slowly drop cash out of her airplane. The money flutters down to the busy streets below like confetti. At first, people did not realize what was raining down on them. Much of the cash fell on the ground while some landed on people's heads. Very quickly, they began to realize what was falling from the sky. The crowded streets and the people started going crazy; grabbing and picking up cash like piranhas in a feeding frenzy. They chased, pushed and fought with each other to grab their share of the falling money. As this was happening, more cash continued to fall from the sky. Money was being littered everywhere. On roof tops of apartment and office buildings to busy sidewalks and heavy traffic streets. People poured into the streets; drivers got out of their cars to pick up money and traffic grind to a halt. Fights and gridlock broke out everywhere. Word of mouth about money falling from the sky spread like a gasoline fire. Soon TV news and radio covered on the event. But their reporting only served to attract more attention and people from elsewhere to midtown; further aggravating the situation. At the same time, Tina continued to drop more money from the sky adding fuel to the fire. Chaos and full blown riots ensued as people fought each other for money. Midtown New York was soon a disaster zone; a scene of greed and madness. Police, fire and every available **first responders** were called to the area to control the rioting crowd.

Back at the Federal Reserve Bank, the five guards that were on duty protecting the Bank heard the call for help on their radio scanners. The guards were at first reluctant to respond because officially, their job was to only guard the Federal Reserve Bank. But there has never been an attempted robbery in the history of the Bank and the call for help sounded too distressing for them not to respond. Amongst the guards, it was decided that four of them would go help with the situation in midtown while one of them would stay behind to guard the Bank. The four responding guards quickly unlocked the Bank's front lobby doors and rushed out. As they did so, Merrill Pynch slipped inside before the doors were locked again.

From the roof of the adjacent building, the Ninja Mice spotted the four guards rushing out of the Bank and into their cars. It was the first and only sign of any activity all night long. Their interest was piqued and they became very concerned. What happened and where were the guards going in such a hurry they wondered. Soon after the guards left the area became quiet again. The mice then realized it was too quiet. In fact, there wasn't any sign of activity, civilians or police anywhere for miles around. Were they wrong about their predicted attack on the Federal Reserve Bank they wondered. Were the rats robbing another bank somewhere else? They were nervous but decided to sit tight for a few more minutes to see what might happen next.

As Merrill slipped inside the Bank, he found the lone guard left behind. His plan was the same as all the previous bank robberies; to **incapacitate** the guard with a sleeping pill. But unlike the other times, there was no cup and the guard here was not drinking anything. Frustrated, Merrill had to come up with another plan or kill the guard and be done with it. He was very tempted by the latter option but knew Goldmouse would not approve. The goal was to rob the Bank and remain undetected. Merrill then came up with a brilliant new plan. He went back to the locked front lobby doors of the Bank where Karl and the other 12 troops of his team were waiting on the other side. Merrill unlocked the doors and went outside to give Karl some very specific instructions. He told Karl to wait two minutes, then knock on the glass door until the guard comes. When the guard comes, Karl is to pretend he is a beautiful woman. He must seduce the guard away from the bank. After giving his instructions, Merrill placed his hand on Karl. Using his Chi Growth powers, Merrill transformed Karl into a human size rat. Afterwards, Merrill went back inside the Bank and locked the front doors again. He then found and snuck up behind the guard where he whispered a very strong mind trick suggestion to him. Merrill said, "There is a very beautiful woman knocking at the door. She is frightened by the riots in midtown. If the words you say are right, she will let you kiss her. You should then escort her home safely."

Moments later, there was indeed a knock on the front doors. The guard walked over to the lobby doors like some sort of zombie. A very gruff and gnarly looking Karl stood nervously on the other side. But to the guard, he saw a beautiful but shy and nervous woman batting her eyelashes. It was love at first sight for the guard. He opened the front doors to welcome Karl in.

"Good evening miss. How can I help you, my beautiful lady?" said the guard. "It's a terrible night to be out alone. Won't you come inside and be with me?"

"Oh, um, uh, err... I'd love to, but I must get home." Karl said nervously as he did his best to speak like a lady. "Umm, I live in midtown and there are riots there right now. Won't you walk me home and keep me safe buddy? err, I mean sir... err, I mean you handsome man, you."

"I'd love to take you home, but I have to stay and guard the Bank. Perhaps you'd like to stay here until after my shift. I can walk you home then. By the way, what's your name, beautiful?"

"Um, err, my name? It's Karr... err, I mean, **Helen**. You can call me Helen. Yeah, my name is Helen..." Realizing he was failing at his assigned mission, Karl cringed and puckered up his lips to kiss the guard. **SMOOOOOOOCH**. The guard was instantly in love. So in love and blinded by Merrill's mind control trick that he didn't even see or feel Karl's scratchy whiskers as they kissed. Moreover, Karl is a cigarette smoking rat. His breath stinks like smoke so kissing him would be like kissing an ash tray. But the guard was oblivious to this as well. Karl on the other hand was gagging and wanted to spit. If the guard had realized he just kissed a dirty disgusting rat, he too would have wanted to spit as well. After they kissed, the guard walked out the Bank hand in hand with Karl to escort him/her home. As they walked out, the Ninja Mice spotted them.

"**Oh My Gosh!!!**" René cried. "It's a gigantic rat holding hands and walking with a guard from the Bank. What the heck!!!" The mice knew right there and then that this was the work of an Asumari Master using the Chi Growth effect of the full moon. They knew the Bank was indeed the target tonight and it is under attack now. But where were Goldmouse, Merrill or the other rats. The mice decided to wait further rather hoping Goldmouse or Merrill will show themselves. Tactically, this was smarter than jumping into a situation where they didn't have all the information on their enemy in terms of their strength or their numbers.

As Karl led the guard away, Merrill opened the doors for the rest of his team of 12 rats. They immediately went to work on locating and dismantling the Bank's security system. It didn't take the rats long. Having done multiple bank robberies for more than two weeks straight, the rats have become quite proficient. After shutting down the security and alarm systems, Merrill used his Chi Force powers to psychically signal to Goldmouse that it was safe to send rest of the rat army up to the Bank. Goldmouse sent all but 20 of the troops up the bank. The 20 rat soldiers that stayed behind had another task to do elsewhere. Goldmouse used his Chi Growth powers to transform them into human sized rats. Merrill and his 12 member team waited for Goldmouse and the rest of the army by the vault elevator on the main floor. As they waited, the 12 rats noticed there were cheese sticks hidden in nooks and crevasses around the elevator. They were the same ones left there by the Ninja Mice earlier and poorly hidden on purpose. Without hesitating or thinking twice, the 12 rats eagerly chowed down. **YUM YUM YUM!!!**

Moments later, Goldmouse arrives at the vault elevator with hundreds of rats soldiers to meet up with Merrill. It was then that Goldmouse and Merrill used the Chi Growth effect of the full moon on themselves and on everyone else. They all transformed from grapefruit sized rats to human sized criminals enabling them to more easily carry and steal the heavy gold from the Bank. Merrill takes most of the troops down to the vault while the rest remained in the lobby with Goldmouse. Merrill's group descend down in groups of 6 as that was all the elevator could hold at once. The process was tedious as the elevator was a slow moving one rather than a modern high speed elevator.

Arriving in the underground vault, Merrill was surrounded by gold bars and coins everywhere he looked. He was eager to start unlocking and dismantling the compartments where the gold was kept. When all members of Merrill's group arrived down at the vault, they went to work immediately; unlocking compartments and carrying out loads of heavy gold. Some used their hands while others used the Bank's forklifts and pallet jacks.

As that was happening, the 12 rats that ate the cheese sticks earlier each began to feel a rumble in their bellies. The 12 looked at each other with regret as they speculated on the cause of their stomach ailment. They felt gassy and distended at first. But the gurglies then came quickly. It hit them fast and hard and they felt a dire need to do a bowel movement. "Uh-oh, this is not good" one of the rats thought to himself. Each of the affected rats was unaware of the severity of the others. But the urgent need to use the toilet caused all 12 of them to immediately drop what they were doing and rush for the elevator. But they soon remembered that the elevator could only hold 6 at a time. For the unfortunate half who hesitated just slightly or were not as quick, they had to wait for the elevator to return. All of them – the 6 in the elevator and the 6 waiting below – crossed their legs and clenched their gluteus maximus tightly to hold back their **intestinal tsunami.**

Once the elevator reached the ground floor with its first load of ailing rats, the door flung open. The 6 rats scurried as quickly as possible to the washroom. It was not easy for them to run with their legs crossed. When they reached the washroom, they found only 4 available toilet stalls. Having learned their lesson from the elevator ride, *'if you snooze, you lose'* the 6 rats scrambled, raced and fought with each other to get into one of the 4 available stalls. Four of them were eventually victorious in their struggle. The unlucky 2 who lost out were in full panic mode at this point as they could not hold it any longer. They pulled and pounded on the stall doors; begging and pleading to be let in even before the occupants had a chance to use the toilet. The unlucky 2 even tried to crawl in underneath to the shock and horror of the stall occupant. **"What the heck! Dude, this is so wrong! Privacy! Get out!"** they yelled and kicked. The unlucky 2 were out of options. But fortunately they were quick thinkers. They darted over next door to the women's washroom and used the ladies toilets to relieve themselves. **"Oh thank goodness,"** they cried.

At the same time, the 4 rats who thought they were lucky soon found out otherwise. They had trouble lifting their toilet lids up as they were taped down tightly. The 4 desperately and franticly tried to lift their lids as they screamed in anguish, **ARRRGGG!!!** But they managed to lift their lids at the very last possible moment and managed not to soil themselves. Lifting their lids, they immediately slammed their butts down on their toilet seats at which point, they simultaneously unleashed their thunderous diarrhea tsunami while exploding the ketchup packs that was taped under their toilet seats. The violent release of intestinal gas and excrement was so loud that it covered up the sound of the exploding ketchup packs which sprayed all over the back of the rats' legs just behind their knees. When they finally realized they were covered in ketchup, the rats just rolled their eyes. At that point, they didn't care anymore. They were just relieved! The rats then went to clean themselves and reached for the toilet paper. At that point, they found their final aggravation. The toilet paper was taped up and they could not unroll or dispense any of it to use. **ARRRGGG!!!**

The last 6 ailing rats came up from the vault slowly. To them the elevator was slower than molasses. They were dying to get out of the elevator. As soon as the door opened, they rushed out and ran for the washroom. With their legs crossed and their butts clenched, they scurried as quickly and as goofy as one might imagine. They desperately reached the washroom only to find all the stalls were occupied. By that point it was far too late as all 6 of them relieved themselves right there on the floor of the men's room. It was the most disgusting and horrid sight and smell you could imagine. **ARRRGGG!!!** The worst part was they knew they would have to clean up the entire mess if they were to leave no evidence or trace of them being at the Bank and robbing it.

The screams of anguish were loud enough to be heard by the Ninja Mice who were still on the roof of the building adjacent to the Bank. And not knowing what was happening inside or who was screaming, the mice prepared to act. But just then, a convoy of 20 school buses drive up to the Bank. The buses were driven by the 20 rats that were left behind in the tunnels and dispatched by Goldmouse for this task. The rat troops from inside the Bank opened the front lobby doors. They came out to the school buses to help unload what looked like gold bars and coins. The Ninja Mice saw all of it happening from the roof adjacent to the Bank. They had seen enough! Using the Chi Growth effect of the full moon, the mice transformed themselves into human size heroes. The Ninja Mice jumped into action; leaping off the roof of the building and landing on top of the school buses. **KA-THOOM...** **KA-THOOM... KA-THOOM... KA-THOOM...**

The sudden sound and sight of ninjas dropping down from the sky and landing the roof of the buses caught the rats by surprise. They instinctively dropped the gold looking cargo they were carrying and braced themselves for a fight. The mice standing on top of the buses had the advantage of being on high ground. Buffy quickly used his enhanced Chi Force powers to create a thick cloud of fog and smoke to shroud himself and the other mice. The rats could not see a thing as the mice attacked them. Knyse knocked out two rats with a series of elbows and knee strikes. Buffy did the same while René was able to defeat three rats with his speed and Tonfas. Soros on the other hand took out four rats soldiers with his superior strength and Bo Staff. In mere moments, the four Ninja Mice were able to defeat eleven vicious rats. The mice then picked up the gold looking cargo that lay on the ground. They soon realized it was not gold at all. Instead, it was actually chocolate that was wrapped with gold tin foil made to look like gold coins and gold bars. The mice also realized the plan must have been to replace the real gold down in the vault with the fake gold that was in the buses. Suddenly, a strong gust of wind blew away the fog and smoke that was shrouding the Ninja Mice. It was Goldmouse Sachs. He was standing in the lobby of the Bank and surrounded by hundreds of rat soldiers. It was the first time in over a year that Goldmouse and the Ninja Mice were standing face to face.

"So you're still alive and up to your old tricks, huh." Knyse said to Goldmouse.

"**ATTACK!**" Goldmouse shouted. "And show them no mercy!" He added. "Merrill, the Ninja Mice are here! Forget the stealth plan. We don't have time for that anymore. Let's just grab the gold and get out of here!" Goldmouse yelled down to Merrill who was still down in the vault. Once he heard this, Merrill ordered all the rats that were down in the vault with him to go and fend off the Ninja Mice.

Hundreds of rat soldiers streamed out of the Bank and rushed towards the Ninja Mice. The mice were badly out-numbered. The only sensible thing to do was to retreat across the street. Once on the other side of the street, the mice created some space between them and the on-coming rats. Buffy once again created a shroud of fog and smoke for the mice to hide inside. The rats, not wanting to charge blindly into the unkrown, stopped in their tracks. They then picked up whatever was nearby and whatever they could get their hands on and threw it **indiscriminately** into the thick fog. Inside the fog, debris rained down on the mice. Knyse used his enhanced Chi Force power to create an umbrella like energy shield to protect himself and the other mice from the smaller falling items like rocks and bricks. The larger and heavier debris thrown at them were batted away by Soros, Buffy and René with their weapons. While the mice remained relatively safe behind Knyse's energy shield, their surroundings were not. The rats could not see where the mice were or what they were throwing things at. As a result, parked cars and nearby office windows were smashed.

While the Ninja Mice were kept at bay by most of the rats troops, Goldmouse, Merrill and a few of the rat soldiers quickly loaded the 20 school buses with the real gold. Goldmouse and Merrill were able to use their Chi Force powers to lift the heavy gold and speed up the vault elevator. The buses were loaded to capacity with nearly 20 million ounces of gold in each. Once they finished, Goldmouse and 20 drivers drove off with the buses. As the buses were slowed by the extreme weight of the gold, Merrill was ordered to stay behind to ensure the Ninja Mice did not follow the escaping convoy of buses.

As Goldmouse made his getaway, Merrill took command of the rat army. Merrill was eager to take on the Ninja Mice and put his abilities to the test. Using his Chi Force powers, he created a gust of wind to blow away the fog, exposing the mice. Soon the Ninja Mice and Merrill locked eyes on each other. Although this was the first time the mice are encountering Merrill Pynch, there was something oddly familiar about him. But the mice could not immediately put their finger on it.

"Prepare to die, you meddling mice!" Merrill yelled.

"Ooooo, mister big and scary is threatening us. We're so scared." Knyse mocked. "What do they call you, number two? I'd say it's nice to meet you, but I have a feeling you're a nasty-nasty #2. We don't like nasty number twos."

"Hey #2, I'm Buffet the Biscuit Thief. But you can call me Buffy. You know, we don't have to fight, right? Why don't you just put the gold back and we can go grab dinner; get to know each other. Nobody needs to get hurt here. What do you say?"

"You will die tonight and I will feast on your flesh and broken bones!" Merrill threatened.

"Don't sing it; bring it sucka!" René countered.

Merrill didn't care for the trash talk. He just wanted to kill the mice. Using his Chi Force, Merrill lifted a heavy office desk from inside the Bank and hurled it at the mice. Knyse drew his Katana and leaped into air to intercept the flying desk. With one quick stroke of his sword, Knyse chopped the desk in half; striking it down. "Is that all you've got," Knyse taunted. He obviously knew it wasn't. But Knyse's taunting was done deliberately to inflame Merrill's rage in the hopes that it would cause him to make a mistake. The taunting certainly did its job as Merrill turned into full rage mode. He levitated everything in the surrounding area that wasn't bolted down; cars, bicycles, mopeds, office furniture, chairs, trash cans, fax machines, photocopiers. Everything floated as if they were weightless in outer space. Merrill hurled all of it at once at the mice who had to scramble for cover. The Mice darted inside one of the office buildings whose windows were smashed earlier by the rat troops. Flying cars and heavy office equipment smashed into the office building, knocking down walls.

The mice were trapped inside the building by collapsing walls and piled up of debris. Damage to the building was extensive. Water mains and natural gas pipelines were also damaged. This caused water to spray uncontrollably. Fire or even an explosion due to the ruptured gas line became a concern. Merrill then ordered his rat troops to swarm the building and finish the mice off. Inside the office building, the Ninja Mice could hear the rats dig their way through the rubble. Knyse then used his Chi Force power to create electro energy sparks. He thrusted the sparks towards the source of the gas leak near the pile of rubble separating them and the rats. The electro energy sparks ignited the gas causing a fiery explosion and blowing a hole in the wall of debris. The mice readied themselves for a fight. Soros picked up a photocopier machine over his head, ready to throw it at the first rat he sees. But as they braced themselves, the mice suddenly heard the sound of wailing sirens. It was the police. And lots of them too.

The commotion and damage done to the surrounding buildings at the beginning of the fight with the rats triggered burglar alarms. As a result, the police were alerted. And when they realized the alarms were coming from nearby buildings around the Federal Reserve Bank, the police responded accordingly by sending as many officers as possible.

Upon hearing the police sirens, Merrill knew there was nothing more that could be gained by staying to fight with the mice or the police. They had succeeded in stealing the gold they came for. Merrill decided to immediately retreat with his troops. The mice heard the rats retreating and realized that it was also best for them to retreat as well. Soros hurled the photocopier that he was holding to smash open a wider hole in the debris wall for them to escape. When the police arrived, they found an entire city block in ruins and the Federal Reserve Bank emptied of its precious gold.

Chapter Eleven
Attack at the Chocolate Factory

The Ninja Mice escaped the burning crime scene by climbing back up to the roof of the building adjacent to the Federal Reserve Bank. There they regrouped to figure out their next move and how they would track down Goldmouse. How far could he have possibly gone with all that heavy gold? And where could he possibly go to hide it all. The mice were scratching their heads trying to figure it out. It's not easy to escape and hide with 20 bus loads of gold. But with Goldmouse's mastery of the Chi Force and help from Merrill Pynch, he could really be anywhere by now.

The police soon arrived on the scene responding to the burglar alarms. They did the predictable thing of forming a perimeter to seal off all entry and exit points in a one block radius around the crime scene. This allowed the police to begin looking for any remaining **perpetrators** that may still be at the scene and also to investigate and collect evidence. It was standard police protocol. The Ninja Mice spied and eavesdropped on the police as they processed the crime scene. The mice hoped to learn something that would help them track down Goldmouse. Soon, a news reporter arrived on the scene to cover on the developing story. It was Walter Leland. While most of the news media were still in midtown New York covering the riots caused by the money falling out of the sky, Walter knew that police responding to an incident near the Federal Reserve Bank would be an important story that needed to be covered. The Ninja Mice saw Walter arrive at the scene and begin talking to the police. They climbed down from their roof top perch and snuck into Walter's news van to wait for him to return.

When Walter finished speaking with the police, he returned to his van. And because it was dark, he did not see the Ninja Mice sitting in the back of his vehicle waiting for him. Nor was Walter looking for or expecting anyone to be inside. As soon as he got in and closed the door, he heard an unexpected voice behind him, "Hey Walt! How's it going?" Buffy said suddenly.

"**D'AHHHH!!!**" Walter screamed. "Mice! You scared the life out of me! What are you doing here? What are you doing in my Van?" Although Walter and the mice are friends, it was still a shocking sight for him, as it would be for anyone, to see four gigantic human sized mice in his back seat.

The mice told Walter what had happened and how Goldmouse and his apprentice, Merrill Pynch, robbed the Bank of all its gold. Walter was horrified to learn this. Walter then told the mice about the riots in midtown caused by money falling from the sky. Together, Walter and the Ninja Mice concluded that the two events had to be related. Goldmouse created and used the riots as a distraction cover for him to rob the Federal Reserve Bank. But the question now is where did he go with all that gold. The mice also told Walter about the fake gold that Goldmouse was going to swap with the real gold in the Bank until they showed up and spoiled his plans. "That must have been a lot of chocolate gold coins and bars." said Walter.

"Twenty bus loads to be exact!" Knyse said.

"Wow! Where would he have gotten all that chocolate from?" Walter wondered. "He could not have stolen it all from a candy store. If he didn't, it would have been reported and I would know about it. There is an old chocolate factory in uptown New York near Hershey Highway. But that place has been closed for years."

The revelation of an old abandoned factory in uptown piqued Knyse's interest. "Hmmm, a chocolate factory you say? It might out of business now, but it's possible that Goldmouse may have secretly been using it to make his fake gold. It sounds like the perfect place to use as a base to plan the biggest heist ever. We have to go check it out!"

The Ninja Mice wasted little time in racing north to find the old abandoned factory in uptown New York. By the time they arrive, it was nearly dawn. The full moon had disappeared from the sky and the mice had returned to their normal size. The factory indeed looked desolate from the outside. It was enclosed by a chain linked fence with posted warning signs stating "**private property**" and "**No trespassing.**" The building itself was old and grey and was surrounded by overgrown weeds. Its windows were boarded up with sheets of plywood. There were no obvious signs of life or activity inside so it would have been natural to assume the old factory was deserted. But when the mice looked more closely, they saw tracks leading in and out of the building.

"Guys, I think we got something here." said Knyse to the others. "Look, there are tire tracks and paw tracks. Keep your eyes open everybody. I think we may have found Goldmouse's hideout."

In their normal rodent size, the Ninja Mice easily walked through the openings in the fence. They carefully approached the old factory using all their senses to stay alert and avoid detection. The mice noticed there were 3 rats patrolling the perimeter of the factory. Two were guarding an entrance door while a third rat was pacing back and forth on the roof. To humans, this would not have looked out of place or raised suspicion. After all, it was just rats hanging out at an abandoned building. What so strange about that? But for the Ninja Mice, they knew they had tracked down Goldmouse's secret base. And they had the element of surprise on their side.

It was decided that Soros would climb to the roof to deal with the rat there while René and Buffy would deal with the two by the door. Knyse on the other hand would keep an eye out for other rats that may be patrolling the factory. Soros climbed up the east side of the building to the edge of the roof. There he paused and waited for the morning sun to rise. As the sun rose from the horizon behind Soros, the rays of sunlight provided cover for him to sneak up on the rat. Soros quickly and quietly neutralized the rat with a swift blow to the back of the rat's head with his Bo Staff. Down on the ground, René and Buffy were hiding behind an empty garbage barrel. Across from them and on the opposite side was Knyse. He was hiding behind an empty pop can. Knyse began tapping on the can with a stone while he squeaked softly like he was injured or in distress. The rats heard the noise coming from Knyse and they went over to investigate. As they did, René and Buffy ran up behind them and knocked them unconscious.

"Good job fellas!" said Knyse. "Now let's tie these guys up and put them in the barrel so no one will find them."

Soros climbed down from the roof to rejoin the others. Together, they found a way into the factory. This inside was as **dilapidated** as was the outside. There the Ninja Mice found the twenty school buses that were used in the gold robbery last night. They looked inside the buses to see if they had anything in it. But the buses were empty. The mice did notice there were skid marks on the floor leading to a freight elevator. They could hear faint sounds through the elevator shaft coming from below the ground floor. The mice knew that if they summon for the elevator, it could alert the rats to their presence. So instead, the mice used the elevator shaft to climb down into the basement levels of the factory. The further down they went, the louder the faint sounds became. The mice had to climb three floor levels down before they found the first opening in the shaft. From there, the mice climbed out through the opening and on to a narrow walkway high above the factory floor. Below them, they saw hundreds, if not thousands, of rats feasting and celebrating. The rats were jubilant and rowdy. Many were dipping and dunking their food into the massive chocolate fountain at the corner of the factory floor. Some even dunked themselves in as they tried to swim in the fountain. Others were drinking and dancing under a shower of root beer that sprayed from punctured cans. The rats were obviously proud of themselves. Fueled by caffeine and euphoria, they must have been partying all night long and into the morning.

"Oh my goodness, that looks like so much fun. And delicious too!" said Buffy referring to rats swimming in the fountain as he looked on with envy. "Maybe we could join them? What do you guys think?"

"Get serious, Buffy. Those rats aren't going to share." said Knyse. "And even if they did, I wouldn't want to eat the chocolate after those dirty rats have been bathing in it. But it does give me an idea. Soros, you're big enough to pass for a rat. If you dunk yourself into that fountain and cover yourself in chocolate, you could pretend to be one of them. Then you'll be able to infiltrate into their ranks and find the stolen gold."

"Are you kidding me?! Soros pushed back at Knyse's suggestion. "No way am I jumping in there and covering myself in chocolate."

"Oh come on, Soros. Do it. Take one for the team." said René.

"I'll do it!" Buffy volunteered.

"No Buffy. You're too small to pass off for a rat." said Knyse. "And if you did, you'll be busy eating the chocolate. We may not see you again for a week. We'll have to think of something else. Hey, what's that over there?!!"

Across from the Ninja Mice on the walkway and in the distance directly in front of them was an office with a balcony. There, the mice noticed a silhouette of a menacing figure in the window. As the mice sensed figure in the window and felt his presence with their Chi Force, the figure sensed them too. It was Merrill Pynch. His office door suddenly flung open. Merrill stood in the door way with his Katana drawn and ready to fight.

"**Attention rat soldiers!**" Merrill yelled down to his troops. "The Ninja Mice are here in the factory! Get up here now!" Merrill added. He then marched confidently towards the mice who readied themselves for a showdown. Knyse drew his Katana and jumped at Merrill Pynch swinging. Their swords **clanged** and **clashed**. The other mice ran behind Merrill to take position. He was surrounded by the mice in a 4 on 1 battle. Merrill swung his

Katana ferociously, clashing with the mice and their ninja weapons. Merrill lunged forward with a straight thrust of his sword to keep Buffy at bay. He then turned to René to deliver an overhead downward strike. René had to react fast to shield and protect himself with his Tonfas pressed against his forearms. Merrill's attention then quickly turned to an incoming Knyse who feinted a swipe with his Katana. That momentary deception allowed Soros to smack Merrill in the back hard with his Bo Staff. Merrill was stunned. Soros paused briefly as he was surprised by his lucky blow. But Merrill retaliated with a sudden Chi Energy punch that came from him thrusting his palm. It hit Soros in the chest knocking him to the ground. Merrill had his back to Buffy at this point. Buffy saw his opportunity. He bravely jumped on to Merrill's back and wrapped his Nunchaku around Merrill's throat, choking him. Merrill struggled and gasped for air. René saw his chance to get up close. He ran right up to Merrill swinging his Tonfas with deadly accuracy. René hit Merrill in the torso with several devastating strikes that would have killed an ordinary opponent. But Merrill was no ordinary adversary. He was fierce and strong. As René wound up for another swing, Merrill punted René like a football. The monstrous kick sent René flying and crashing through ceiling lights. Merrill then reached behind his head to grab Buffy by the back of his neck and shoulder. With a quick jerk forward, Merrill threw Buffy off his back. The throw sent Buffy crashing into the balcony rails, crushing the railings as he landed. Knyse ran to check on his friends. The mice regrouped behind Knyse who readied himself to take on Merrill in a deadly sword duel. But Merrill had other ideas as he began to rip things from the floor and off the walls to throw at the mice. The mice were able to block or deflect much of it with their Chi Force powers. But the situation was becoming **perilous**. They decided to retreat from the fight with Merrill as they saw the tremendous number of rats heading their way up the staircase. Merrill then also retreated as he went back inside his office.

The mice were now stuck between Merrill in his office and the rat troops running up the stairs. The mice decided to face the rats at the top of the stairway as they came up. This gave the mice the advantage of being on high ground. The rats on the other hand had the disadvantage of being stuck in a bottleneck narrow stairway. The first rats to arrive at the top had the misfortune of getting whacked in the head by the mice. The rats at the front of the line had no choice but to take their beating because they could not stop or take a step back. When they tried, the rats at the back just pushed the ones at the front forward and up the stairs. For a while there, it was fun for the mice. They smacked and whacked the rats like oversized piñatas. And no matter how hurt or injured the mice were from their fight with Merrill, they knew they could not let up. If enough of the rats were to make it all the way up to the walkway, the mice would eventually be overwhelmed and lose to the rats by their sheer numbers.

Back at the office, Merrill was on the phone with Goldmouse who was at his secret hideout. Merrill informed Goldmouse that the

Ninja Mice had found them and were attacking the factory. Goldmouse ordered Merrill to evacuate the factory immediately and to take as much of the loot as possible.

"Get out of there now!" Goldmouse ordered. "The police could be on their way. Kill the mice if you can. But that is not the main goal. We need to safeguard and move as much of the loot as possible before the cops show up. Start with the cash and jewels. Then take as much gold as you can."

As the Ninja Mice were still busy whacking every rat that came up the stairs, Merrill's office suddenly door flung open again. Merrill hesitated to leave. He wanted to stay and fight the mice; hoping to destroy them once and for all. But Merrill had his orders. He fearlessly jumped over the balcony rails. Merrill landed safely on the factory floor below amongst his troops. The mice were exhausted by this point and saw their opportunity to retreat into Merrill's office. As they did so, hundreds of rats flooded up the stairway. The mice barricaded themselves in Merrill's office. They pushed a heavy desk up against the door and turned a table on to its side to fortify the window. The table was reinforced with heavy filing cabinets.

"Well, that was kind of fun whacking those rats." René said half-jokingly and out of breath.

Trying to sound confident and reassuring to his comrades, Knyse said, "Yeah, it kind of was fun. Maybe we'll get a chance to do it again later."

"I think we might get a chance to do it again sooner rather than later." Buffy added nervously. "I don't think there's another way out of here except through that door. What are we going to do if those rats manage to break down the door?"

"Not a chance." Soros said optimistically. "That door is solid and the desk is pretty heavy. Let's just relax, hang-out and sing some songs together."

"Oh, that's a great idea, Soros." Knyse said with a brave face who then led the mice in a song:

We'll be safe inside our office when they come...
We'll be safe from creeps and killers when they come...
Un--less they have a blow torch or a poison gas injector,
Then we'll have to kick their butts again when they come

We'll be safe inside our office when they come...
We'll be safe from creeps and killers when they come...
Un--less they have some sort of thermal nuclear bomb,
Then we're all be dead so that's really dumb
(Repeat)

While the mice sang their little song, the rat troops continued to pound on the fortified door as they tried to break it down. The mice tried to keep their spirits up by using humor. "Hey rats... how do like our song?" René asked rhetorically. "If you didn't like that one, we've got another one for you!"

1 - 2 - 3 - 4 Ready for a bloody war
5 - 6 - 7 - 8 You're a smelly fish bait

René: "Or how about this one..."
3 - 5 - 7 - 9 We're gonna break your spine
René: "Okay, one more..."
2 - 4 - 6 - 8 Who do we appreciate
The rats, the rats... Rah Rah Rah
Flush them down the toilet... Ha Ha Ha

As the Ninja Mice huddled and sang to comfort themselves, the light in their office flickered. An image of Goldmouse Sachs then appeared on the office wall. It came from a video conference projector. Goldmouse came on live video to speak to the mice.

"So Ninja Mice, I see my rat soldiers have you trapped inside Merrill's office. Sooner or later, they will break down that door. And when they do, they will crush you!"

"Hey Goldilocks... How you doing? We haven't seen you in over a year. Why didn't you write or call us? Didn't you miss us? Knyse teased. "By the way smarty pants, what are your plans with all that gold?" Knyse added knowing how Goldmouse likes to brag about his plans and talk about himself.

"I'm going to take over the world! For too long, a small number of people and a few countries have ruled the world with their economic might. Their powers were created by an oppressive economic structure and supported by corrupt and fraudulent business practices. Wealth and resources have been stolen from the rest of world through dishonest means; creating huge income inequality. Those at the top of the wealth ladder with the most resources stayed at the top while keeping the rest of the world in debt and economic slavery. Economic power and prosperity of the top 1% have built global economies dependent on money and backed by gold. Now I have their gold and money. I have their wealth and power! And with my Chi Force powers, I will rule the world! Everyone will soon be my slave employee! I will be the most powerful Asumari ever. No one will ever threaten or dare to compete with me. I will destroy any Asumari who dares to try."

"You??? Take over the world?" Knyse mocked. "No way... You're Goldmouse Sucks! You suck at taking over the world. And you also suck at explaining yourself... **blah, blah, blah**... Just say you're a greedy bugger and you stole money."

"**How dare you insult me like that?!!!**" Goldmouse was seething mad. "I do not suck! I am an Asumari Grandmaster! I am a criminal mastermind! I'm an **EVIL GENIUS!!!**"

The mice all looked each other and chuckled. They then taunted Goldmouse with an insulting chant to further **antagonize** him...

You're an evil genius
With a tiny little "BLEEP"
Your mother is from Venus
You like to watch Star Trek;
Pretend you're a Klingon
You like to hang around Uranus

Dear young readers:
The authors of this book felt the word that rhymes with genius may be inappropriate so it was bleeped out. But if you managed to figure out what that word is... well, congratulations. You are very smart. But don't tell your parents, okay? :)

"**ARRRGGG!!!** You mice think you're funny. Well guess what! I'm going to have the last laugh. I know where your secret dojo is. And I also know about your girlfriends at the candy store. Once my rats remove all the gold from the factory and relocate it somewhere else safe, I'm going to kill your precious Grandmaster Greenspan. And I'm going to kill your girlfriends. I'm going to destroy all that is dear to you!"

"So the gold is still here at the factory, huh?" said Knyse. "Thanks for telling us it's still here, dumb-dumb. What about the money and jewels? Are they here too?" Knyse razzed. "It's a good thing we brought a bomb with us. We'll going to have to blow up this factory and bury all the stuff you stole here. Good luck moving the gold when it's under a pile of cement rubble and when the place is crawling with police."

GRRRRRRR Goldmouse was flipping mad as he ended the video call abruptly. His threats have the Ninja mice very concerned. In addition, Buffy was also confused. "We brought a bomb with us? Really?" he asked. "I hope you're not referring to my gassy gut." Buffy added.

"No, not really." said Knyse. "Art of deception my friend; I was lying about having a bomb. But Goldmouse doesn't know that. Hopefully, my lie will throw him off his plans."

"We cannot stay here and wait for those rats to break through." said Soros. "And we also can't let those rats move the gold out of here either. We need to get out of here to stop them and stop Goldmouse."

"Yeah, I completely agree!" said Buffy. "But how are we going to get out of this office without playing piñata again?"

"Would this help?" asked René as he pulled something out from his pocket. It was the four left over alkali metals they got from the Flea Market. "I was saving it in case there was an opportunity to use it in some sort of prank."

"René, you're always so prepared!" Kynse said excitedly. "This is so awesome I could kiss you! We may not have a bomb, but this is the next best thing. Remember how powerful the sodium metal was and how big the blast was when I blew up our toilet? I say we use the potassium metal to blast the door open and scare away those rats. Then we make a run for it."

"Yes, that's a great idea. Let's do it." said René. "We'll still have the rubidium, cesium and francium afterwards. We could use the remaining metals to blow up this factory so it can never be used again."

"Yes, I agree." said Knyse. "And if they haven't moved all the gold out of here yet, blowing up the factory would also bury the remaining gold and keep it safely out of the rats' dirty paws."

"Uh, guys… Those are great ideas. But I think we have a slight problem." said Buffy. "We don't have any water. How are we going to blast the door open if we don't have any water?"

"Oh that's an easy solve." said René. "We can pee into a cup and then drop the potassium into the cup. Did you know that pee is mostly water?"

"**Eeewww**, that's gross." Soros objected. "Think about the mess that's going to make. Do you really want pee to rain down on us when the blast goes off?"

"No, but it'd be funny to have it rain on the rats though." René replied.

"I have a better idea." Soros countered. "There's a fire sprinkler just above the door. We can just break that to release water from the sprinkler. Then we just throw the potassium into the water and blast our way out."

"Yeah, that's a good idea." René said agreeably. "But I still have to pee. I forgot to do a *just-in-case* pee when we left the bank."

While René went to water the plants in Merrill's office, the rest of the Ninja Mice pushed all the remaining heavy furniture in the office together to form a protective bunker. Once everything was in place, Soros used his brute strength to break the fire sprinkler. Water gushed out over the office door as the mice hid behind their newly built bunker. René could not resist throwing one last taunt at the rats before they blew the door open. **"Hey rats... are you guys hungry**? We're coming out and we've got eight knuckle sandwiches to share. Who wants to be first?" René then threw the potassium into the gushing water...

The door and half the wall blew apart in a loud **concussive** ball of fire. The blast sent the rats that were near the door flying. The rats that were further away were scared off by the blast and the deafening sound. The Ninja Mice ran out from their bunker feeling victorious.

"Who's hungry?" René taunted. "Step right up and come get your knuckle sandwiches! We've got a limited quantity so some of you are going to have to share!"

"And if you're not hungry for knuckle sandwiches, we've got all you can eat alkali bombs." Knyse added. "Bigger ones too... The last one was just potassium. Same stuff that's found in bananas. They're high in potassium in case you rats didn't know. Rubidium, cesium and francium are going to be a lot more fun."

The rats had no idea what Knyse was talking about. It all sounded too scientific and scary for them so they scurried away in fear. "You rats better run! We're going to blow up the entire factory! RUN!!!" Knyse shouted like a maniac.

"Okay, now what?" Buffy asked. "How are we going to blow up the factory without blowing ourselves up? We need a source of water for the alkali metals to react with. But if we simply throw it into the water sprinkler here at the office, we're all dead meat!"

"You're right Buffy." Soros said. "We need some sort of timer or somehow get the alkali metals to react more slowly to give us time to get far away from the factory."

"I've got it!" Kynse yelled. "The chocolate fountain! We'll toss the metals into the fountain so that they'll be coated in chocolate. Then we'll flood the fountain with water from the fire sprinklers. Once the chocolate coating is dissolved by the water, KA-BOOM!"

"Brilliant idea, Knyse!" said Soros.

René then chimed in to say, "For an added extra punch, we could find and rupture the factory's natural gas lines to fill the factory up with explosive gas."

"Devilishly brilliant little buddy!" said Soros.

"Okay, let's do this!" Knyse said as he tossed the remaining alkali metals down into the chocolate fountain. "Soros, you get ready to flood the fountain with water. The three of us will go find and break the gas lines. When I give you the word, GO, you break the sprinklers. We'll have to run for our lives after that."

Soros climbed up to the ceiling above the chocolate fountain. He quickly found a fire sprinkler head. There Soros gripped it tightly and waited for Knyse's signal to break and release the water. His friends on the other hand had to climb down to the factory floor to locate the natural gas lines. It did not take them long to do so. Once they found the lines, the mice quickly hacked and chewed through them. Explosive gas hissed furiously from the broken lines as it filled up the factory. Knyse then signaled to Soros to do his part. As soon as Soros broke the sprinkler, he quickly joined his friends to flee. By this point, the scene at the factory was chaotic. Because of the potassium explosion earlier, the rats ran to avoid the mice wherever the mice went. The rats all fled in fear as though the mice were like sharks swimming towards a school of fish; the rats gave the mice a wide berth in every direction they went. But the hissing sound and the smell of natural gas in the air only added to the frantic scene as mice and rats alike fled the factory. Moments later... BOOM!

Chapter Twelve
Attack at the Ninja Mice Dojo

The blast at the chocolate factory demolished the building. But Merrill Pynch had escaped earlier with the stolen cash and jewels before the collapse. The rat troops who remained behind were supposed to evacuate the gold. But there was too much and not enough time to move it all. The explosion buried much of the stolen loot. Goldmouse was furious when he learned of this from the rats that had fled the scene. He knew it was not possible to recover his precious gold as the blast site would soon be filled with police and fire officials. By the time he got the news, Goldmouse had already set in motion his plans to attack the United Candy Nations store and the Ninja Mice dojo.

At the United Candy Nations store, Nadia and Diana were having a normal mid-morning. But business at their shop still had not returned to their pre-robbery levels. The store has new display cases, but they are mostly empty as inventory is still lacking. Prior to the robbery, Nadia and Diana were more relaxed and easy going. They were never stressed or anxious at the store. But now, they are more vigilant and alert for danger and thieves. As they waited for customers, Nadia and Diana watched the news on TV. The only thing the TV reporters talked about was the riots last night in New York and the money that fell from the sky. It was very upsetting for the girls to hear how people behaved last night just because of money. The lack of decency, consideration, care or kindness to one another was too depressing. Nadia decided to step away from behind the counter to walk around the store. As she walked by the store window, she noticed a gang of rats fast approaching the store. Nadia's fight-or-flight response kicked in immediately. Her adrenaline started pumping. "**DIANA!**" she yelled. "**RATS ARE COMING!**"

Diana reacted quickly. She grabs a baseball bat from behind the counter and throws it to Nadia, who catches it like a pro. The first two rats to burst into the store got quite the welcome from Nadia. **THUMP!** Into the gut of the first rat. **THUMP!** Again into the second rat as he walked through the door. Then, **WHACK, WHACK** – on their shins; **SMASH, SMASH** – on their feet; and **BASH, BASH** – over their heads. Nadia belted and bashed the rats like she was swinging for a home run. The rats screamed in agony and writhed in pain. But Nadia had no time to celebrate as more rats pushed their way into the store. "**DIANA! MORE RATS ARE COMING**" she yelled.

Nadia's quick actions with the baseball bat gave Diana enough time to run to the back of the store and grab their Nerf guns. Nadia ran behind the counter to join Diana as she took aim at the rats that barged through the door. **Tatt-Tatt-Tatt-Tatt-Tatt-Tatt-Tatt-Tatt-Tatt-Tatt-Tatt-Tatt**. Diana shot wildly with her Stryfe, a battery powered semi-automatic Nerf gun loaded with a 25 dart drum. Rats 3 and 4 who came through the door were peppered with gun shots. They were hit in the face and torso with foam darts that felt like a stiff punch combined with a bee sting.

"Take that you dirty rats!" Diana yelled at the top of her voice as she fired more shots at rats 3 and 4. **Tatt-Tatt-Tatt-Tatt-Tatt-Tatt-Tatt-Tatt-Tatt-Tatt**. Rats 3 and 4 took cover behind rats 1 and 2 as all four cowered in fear. "Who's next?!" Diana yelled; almost daring more rats to storm into the shop that were, at the moment, waiting outside for the shots to let up before rushing in. Diana fired again to keep the first four rats pinned down. **Tatt-Tatt-Tatt - CLICK, CLICK, CLICK...** "Oh-no, I'm out of darts!" Diana cried.

But while Diana kept the rats at bay with her Stryfe, it gave Nadia time to load a couple of guns for herself. When the rats that were waiting outside heard Diana run out of ammo, they charged in. But only three managed to make it inside before Nadia jumped out from behind the counter with her Nerf Rampage loaded with a 12 dart clip. **Pow-Pow-Pow-Pow-Pow-Pow-Pow-Pow-Pow**. She shot the three new rats that managed to get into the store, hitting them with rapid slam-fire. The shots hit them all over their bodies leaving painful welts everywhere. Each hit felt like you were getting cracked by a bamboo stick or whip by a leather belt. Now there were 7 rats writhing and moaning in pain. The brief pause of gun fire allowed another rat to peek in from the outside.

Pow-Pow-Pow - Click, Click, Click... The three shots hit the apprehensive 8th rat in the face. "Waah, my eye! You hit my eye." the rat cried as he clutched his face in pain.

"I'm out!" Nadia yelled to Diana who had ran to the back of the store to retrieve more arsenals for their battle. As that was happening, two more new rats rush in thinking the worst of the gun fire was over. Nadia dropped her Rampage and picked up the second gun she had loaded earlier; the Nerf RotoFury with its 10 devastating mega darts. "Say hello to my little friend!" Nadia said with bad intentions as she fired off a couple of shots. The mega darts whistled passed the two rats, just missing their heads. **BAM-BAM!** The ear shattering sound of the darts smacking against the door behind them was enough to give them chills down their spine. **CHA-CHOOK**, Nadia cocked her Nerf gun and slam-fired the remaining eight mega darts at the rats, hitting them all over. Mega darts are four times the size of normal darts and hit four times as hard. If normal darts hit like a stiff punch, then mega darts hit like a sledgehammer. The rats cried for mercy. Lucky for them, Nadia was out of ammo again.

The last and final rat then burst into the store. It was Boss Rat (AKA, Killer Karl the Rat), leader of the Nabisco Gang. He was very angry at the fact that he and the rest of his rat goons had failed so miserably thus far at taking out a couple of mice; girls no less! How utterly embarrassing and humiliating this would be to his reputation as a menacing gang leader and how disappointed will

Goldmouse be if he fails the mission. Karl shouted at his goons to get up and fight on. "Don't you dare let these girls beat you!" he yelled. "Get them now. Show them no mercy!" Karl added.

As Karl rallied his goons to get up and fight, Diana prepared her final Nerf gun, the Rhino-Fire. This bad boy is a battery powered motorized double-barrel rapid fire fully automatic assault gun mounted on a tripod. It can blast and empty its 50 dart capacity in under 30 seconds; an insane amount of darts. As Karl and his goons charged at the girls, Diana fired on them. She blasted them mercilessly. **Blam-Blam-Blam-Blam-Blam-Blam...** There was nowhere for the rats to hide. **...Blam-Blam-Blam-Blam...** She continued to pummel and beat the rats into submission. All of them, including Karl, yelped and squealed like babies. "You're not so tough are you, mister big bad bossy rat?!" Diana mocked and taunted. **...Blam-Blam-Blam-Blam, Click, Click...** "Uh-oh." Diana whisper quietly as her heart sank. She realized she was out.

The reprieve from the pounding gave Karl a moment of hope. He gathered himself to catch his breath. Huffing and puffing, he yells, "**We're going to get you now!**" But despite his threat on behalf of the others, only Karl rushed at the girls. The other rats had had enough. They've taken more than their fair share of the beating and they called it quits. Diana was terrorized and frozen in place by the snarling beast, Karl, charging at her. She closed her eyes and braced herself for impact. But fortunately, Nadia grabbed a hand full of thumb tacks from under the counter and threw them onto the floor in from them. As Karl rushed at the girls, he ended up stepping on the tacks, piercing and puncturing his tender feet. "**Ow-ow-ow-ow-ow-ow-ow!!!**" he cried.

Nadia and Diana then quickly looked around to see what else they could use to defend themselves. Diana grabbed some eggs and tomatoes from her lunch. She pelted Karl as he hopped around clutching his feet and wincing in pain. The eggs and tomatoes didn't really hurt him. They just embarrassed him and further inflamed his anger. Fortunately, Nadia found something a little more useful. She found a toilet plunger from the washroom. She was going to whack Karl with it, but thought, why not try firing it with the RotoFury? Nadia picked up her gun, cocked it and loaded the plunger in. **BA-BAM!** She shot the plunger at Karl, hitting him in the face. The plunger ended up suctioning on to Karl's face tightly.

GGRR-MMM-GGRR-MMM-AARRGG... Karl moaned and groaned; he stumbled and mumbled as he struggled to pull the plunger off his face.

As that was happening, the Ninja Mice arrived at the candy store as soon as they could. They came directly from the chocolate factory after they blew it up. The mice feared for Nadia and Diana's well-being after Goldmouse threatened to kill them. They expected to find the girls in danger, but hoped for the best. The mice stormed into the candy store with their weapons drawn and ready to fight. "We're here! We're here!" they shouted as they came through the door hoping the sound of their voice would reassure the girls and scare away any would be thugs.

"**AAAAHHGG!**" the rats screamed like terrorized children at the sight of the Ninja Mice. "Save us! Save us!" they shouted to the mice. "Those girls are killers! Save us! Save us!" they added as they fled the store in a hurry. The Ninja Mice were shocked and dumbfounded at what they just witnessed. Did a gang of rats just run to them for help? Did they beg for protection from the girls? What the heck? The mice just stood there looking at each other with their mouths hanging open. They then noticed a humongous rat stumbling around the store with a toilet plunger stuck on his face. *What the heck is he doing*, they asked themselves. Was he kissing and making out with the plunger or something? **Eeewww**, that's gross! No wonder rats have a reputation for being dirty creatures. René then walked up to the massive rat to help him pry off the plunger. It came off with a pop. The rat could not immediately speak as he struggled to catch his breath. He stared at René, feeling thankful at first. But he soon realized that he was surrounded by the four Ninja Mice.

"Heyyyy, don't I know you?" said René with scorn and suspicion. "Aren't you that guy who punched my fist with his face?"

"**AAAAHHGG!**" Karl screamed as he ran from the store in terror. Nadia and Diana then looked up from behind the counter where they were hiding. They felt relieved and grateful when they saw the Ninja Mice. Soros ran to Diana to comfort and check on her. Nadia runs to Knyse and jumps into his arms. "You saved us!" she cried. "You're my hero." Nadia added. Then without thinking or hesitating, she gives Knyse a big long kiss **SMOOOOOOOCH.** After the kiss, Nadia suddenly stopped as she realized what she had just done. Knyse also paused as the kiss took him by surprise, but he wasn't complaining. They stared at each other awkwardly as they both blushed and smile coyly. Knyse then realized that he kind of liked it. The kiss made him feel heroic.

"Oh, that's so sweet." Buffy said referring to Knyse and Nadia's awkward moment display of affection. "I hate to break up this romantic moment, but we must go help Grandmaster Greenspan before it's too late." he added.

"Yes, you're right!" Knyse replied. "I'm sorry we can't stay to help you girls clean up. We have to go help Grandmaster. We believe Goldmouse is launching an attack on him back at the dojo."

"Oh my gosh." Nadia cried. She and Diana were horrified to learn of Goldmouse and his plan to attack Greenspan. "Go! But please be careful and come back to us safely." Nadia added.

The Ninja Mice take off in a hurry. As they rush out, René decided to tease Knyse with a little song that's usually heard sung on playgrounds by children to tease new couples and young love...

Knyse and Nadia;
Sitting in a tree
K-I-S-S-I-N-G
First comes love;
Then comes marriage
Then comes baby
In a baby carriage

Knyse was miffed, but he had no come back. The only thing he could do was growl and stew on getting even later as he was completely flustered and at a loss for words.

"Looks like you'll be going on a shopping date to the mall soon!" René teased further. "You'll have plenty of time then to think of a witty come back, he-he-he." René laughed.

"Don't worry buddy, shopping isn't all that bad." said Soros as he tried to be a supportive friend. "Depending on who you're with, it can actually be fun. And we can be shopping buddies and hang out together at the mall now, too."

Knyse appreciated Soros' optimistic sentiment, but he just rolled his eyes. "René, you're so funny... you should quit being a ninja and become a professional comedian." said Knyse. "And Soros... let's not talk about this right now... or ever. I HATE SHOPPING!"

At the dojo, news of last night's riots has caused Grandmaster Greenspan great distress. He is in a quiet room with a hot cup of tea doing his morning meditations. The fragrance of his tea fills the room. Greenspan focuses on his breathing – slow and deep – while listening to his own heartbeat. He can hear the slightest sounds around him. His peace and calm is suddenly interrupted by a heighten sense of danger. Greenspan feels the presence of intruders and other Chi Force sensitive Asumaris. They sense his presence too. Greenspan opens his eyes and readies himself for battle with his tea and a paper fan. The doors to Greenspan's room slid open and there stood before him was his former student, Goldmouse Sachs.

"Goldmouse!" said Greenspan. "Thou art still alive. I can't sayeth that I am surprised."

"Greenspan, my old master… I've come to finish you once and for all." said Goldmouse. "And when you're gone, you won't be able to continue teaching your darling Ninja Mice. They are too weak and not yet fully trained to stop me. There will be no one left to stop me from ruling the world."

"Evil, thy name is Goldmouse. Tis the reason I ceased teaching thee long ago." said Greenspan. "Thou greed and lust for power shall, in the end, destroy thee. But what makes thou thinketh thou can defeat ye this time."

"I have grown stronger and have learned much more in the years since you stopped teaching me." said Goldmouse. "My powers have nearly doubled since the last time we fought. And you are now more frail and older than ever. But more importantly, I did not come alone."

With that said, a massive serpent then slithered out from behind Goldmouse. It was Madolf Hissler, the evil Asumari spitting king cobra and leader of the Snake Syndicate. He was followed by his gang members Dickie, George and Blair. With the addition of the snakes, the situation became a 5 on 1 battle. Greenspan was a bit confused. He did not have any particular grievances with Madolf. "Why art thou helping Goldmouse?" he asked.

"Because he has promised me a lot of money." Madolf replied.

Then without warning, Madolf suddenly shot a stream of venom at Greenspan. But the old mouse reacted swiftly by blocking the spray with his paper fan. Greenspan then used his Chi Force powers to fill the room with a thick dark smoke. He then wisely retreated deep into the fog to wait for the intruders to come to him. Greenspan and his adversaries could not see each other. But the three Asumaris could sense one another with their Chi Force powers. The powerless snakes, Dickie, George and Blair, on the other hand had no clue where anyone was. But that didn't stop George and Blair from attacking wildly. They blindly rushed into the fog and struck at anything they thought was moving. But all they hit were fog and smoke. Greenspan easily sidestepped every one of their strikes. He then stood right in the middle between George and Blair and said "I'm right here boys." to get their attention. The two snakes instinctively reacted by immediately striking in the direction of Greenspan's voice. Their mouths were wide open ready to clamp down with their fangs like a spring loaded trap as soon as they touched anything. But all they struck were each other. Their faces smashed together and the snakes knocked each other silly. Greenspan then used Chi Force powers to grab George and Blair. He flung them across the room smashing them against the wall of the dojo.

Unlike his snake friends, Dickie was much more calculating. He slithered into the fog cautiously. Dickie flicked his forked tongue in and out to taste the air around him to track down Greenspan. But Dickie could not locate his prey. Greenspan then calmly appeared in front of Dickie; slowly revealing himself from the fog. Dickie coiled himself up for an attack. Greenspan stood still and waited for Dickie to strike. He held his fan opened in one hand and used it to cover his other hand. As Dickie lunged forward to strike, Greenspan threw his tea into Dickie face. The scolding hot tea blinded Dickie. He screamed and writhed in pain; stumbled and trashed into things. Greenspan then took his ceramic cup and smashed it over Dickie's head.

The thick fog then cleared; revealing Greenspan, Goldmouse and Madolf. Greenspan locked eyes with them as he prepared to take on his nemeses. "Thy snakes were common thugs and no match for me. Why bother?" asked Greenspan.

"They were merely a test to see if you could even still fight. You are not as strong as you once were." Madolf replied. "Now let's see how you do against the two of us." he added as his eyes began to sparkle with static electricity. They turned red as Madolf charged up for an energy blast. Meanwhile, Goldmouse held up his hands like the talons of a hawk ready to strike. His hands glowed as he charged up to blast Chi Force energy.

ZAP - ZAP - POW - BOOM - BLAST - WHAM!

Goldmouse and Madolf hurled energy blast at Greenspan who had to duck and dodge as best he could to avoid the destructive strikes. Greenspan wisely realized that using brute force against two powerful adversaries was not a winning strategy. So instead of trading blasts with his foes, he ran to dungeon where there was more cover and weapons to use. Goldmouse and Madolf chased after Greenspan but they lost sight of him in the dimly lit dungeon. The intruders were reluctant to rush in recklessly. They were wary of hidden traps or a potential ambush by Greenspan. Goldmouse and Madolf walked guardedly as they pursued the old mouse. They fired powerful Chi Energy blasts periodically to threaten and to show just how deadly they were. But one could argue they were simply scared and firing random blasts into the dark was their way of reassuring themselves. "You cannot hide from us forever." Goldmouse declared harshly. "Sooner or later, we will find you. **AND. WE. WILL. DESTROY. YOU.**"

"If thou hath come to kill me now, then thou art unwise or thou doth not seeketh to gain me powers for thyself." Greenspan observed.

"What are you talking about you stupid old mouse!" Goldmouse shouted angrily. "Speak normal English and not your ancient and best forgotten relic of a language!"

"I suppose you do not know that if an Asumari perishes during the night of a full moon, the powers of the deceased may be transfer to another Asumari." said Greenspan in modern english. "The full moon was last night. Kill me now, you shall not gain my powers. There is so much I did not teach you; thankfully. You still have much to learn. You are my most regrettable student ever."

"Is this true?" Goldmouse whispered to Madolf.

"You didn't know?" Madolf hissed. "Of course it's true. How do you think I became as powerful as I am now? The powers of the dead cannot be taken from them simply by killing them. Your Chi Force energy must be telepathically connected before the death occurs in order for the transfer to take place. But this talk of gaining Greenspan's powers is pointless. He will never willingly link his Chi Force energy to yours. He is telling you this to belittle you and make you feel dumb so that you second guess yourself. I'm just here to help you kill him and get my cut of your profits."

"I don't care about your insignificant powers. They mean nothing to me." Goldmouse asserted. "I have thousands of rat soldiers at my command and billions of dollars at my disposal. I already have the power and the money to take over the world. Now show yourself and prepare to die."

"Methinks the rat doth protest too much." said Greenspan. He then used his telepathic powers to project his presence and his voice throughout the dungeon room. Goldmouse and Madolf saw flashes of Greenspan and heard him saying, "*I am here! I am here!*" It seemed as though Greenspan was everywhere all at once. Deception is a favourite trick of an Asumari. Goldmouse and Madolf countered by channelling their powers to shake the dungeon voilently. It felt as though there was an earthquake in the room. The walls and the floor began to crack and tremble causing Greenspan to abandon his trickery. Madolf then spotted Greenspan who ran for the obstacle course to seek cover. Madolf chased after him and Goldmouse quickly followed.

"Follow me if thou dare." Greenspan challenged his rivals. "Finish the course in two mintues if thee can. Survive if I alloweth thee." Greenspan then swiftly scaled up a 100 tail tall climbing wall. But unlike most climbing walls, the hold parts that you'd grab and step onto were made of boxing gloves that randomly punch outwards from the wall. For someone as old as Greenspan, he was remarkably agile and quick. But it was all due to his connection to the Chi Force. Madolf was able to slither up the wall unscathed. His long slender snake body allowed him to avoid the punches thrown by the boxing glove holders. Goldmouse was not far behind. But half way up – **WHAM, WHAM, WHAM,** – three stiff jabs rocked him in the face, the stomach and the groin. The shots sent Goldmouse crashing down to the ground.

At the top of the wall, Madolf faced a steep waterslide tube that would take him down to continue with the obstacle course. He decided not to wait for Goldmouse and jumped into the slide instead. Madolf zipped down the tube which flattened out at the bottom. As he exited, he went crashing through a set of bowling pins going faster than Buffy eating a cupcake. Madolf was dazed and disorientated. He paused to collect his thoughts and get his bearings. As Madolf stood there, Goldmouse came zipping down the slide and crashed into him. The crash sent the two of them stumbling forward. They then found themselves standing on one end of a seesaw. Suddenly, a heavy sandbag fell from the ceiling of the dungeon. It came crashing down on the other end of the seesaw they were standing on. The crash launched Goldmouse and Madolf into the air and they were then peppered with Nerf gun shots. Greenspan had finished the course and was manning the Nerf guns. He shot Goldmouse and Madolf mercilessly with a barrage of painful mega darts as they were tossed into the air.

The shots distracted them from using their powers so they crash landed hard. As Goldmouse and Madolf picked themselves up, a flash of bright light blinded them. The distraction allowed a heavy sandbag to come swinging in like a wrecking ball. The sandbag smashed into the two of them and sent them flying across to the other side of the dungeon. Goldmouse and Madolf were battered and beaten.

"Thou hath not completeth ye obstacle course. Thou needeth more time to finish ye course?" Greenspan inquired. As he spoke, Greenspan suddenly felt the presence of another Asumari. It was Merrill Pynch. He came to help Goldmouse after he had safely relocated the cash and jewels from the chocolate factory.

"Enough with trickery and disception. It's time to fight like a real Asumari warrior." said Merrill as he walked into the dungeon to face Grandmaster Greenspan.

As Merrill Pynch entered the room, Greenspan recognized the familiar Chi Force energy that surrounded the figure that stood at the entrance way. "Darryl." he said.

"That name has no meaning for me anymore." Merrill replied. "Darryl Lynch is dead. There is only Merrill Pynch and I am he."

"What have thou becometh?" asked Greenspan as he did not recognize the physical form that stood before him.

"I've become more powerful than I could ever imagine." Merrill replied. "I have become what I have always meant to be; a great and powerful Asumari. The weak and powerless ordinary being that was Darrly is no more."

"Great and powerful thou art; an Asumari thou art not." insisted Greenspan.

"I shall complete my training by destroying you, Greenspan. The rank and title of Asumari is a mere formality at this point." Merrill argued. "Once we destroy you, we shall rule the world."

"No Merrill, thou doth not needeth more training on how to fight and destroy. Nor doth thou needeth training on how to hate. Slayeth me thou may, but it shall not make thou more great nor thou training complete." Greenspan explained. "And why must thou slayeth me? Bloodshed is not required to be an Asumari."

"Because you and your precious Ninja Mice stand in our way of taking over the world. You defend everyone indiscriminately; the rich, the poor, the wealthy, the weak, the strong, the educated and the ignorant, you defend them all. Even the unscrupulous and cruel ones who deserve to be punished, you give them mercy instead. Because of this, you stand in my way of getting even with those who killed my family. The pain of losing them haunts me greatly. I will inflict the pain I bear on all my enemies."

"Not all humans and not all in New Mouse City art thou enemy deserving of punishment. Attacks on all is a mask for greed and power and fully unjust. What happened to thy family twas a most unfortunate tragedy, but an unintentional one. Goldmouse hath failed thee and led thee down a dark path." Greenspan warned.

"No! Master Goldmouse has made me everything I am today. He recognized my potential when no one else even bothered to give me a chance. He gave me work when I lost my job. He rescued me and took my under his guidance. He has given the powers to seek retribution and vengence upon those who killed my family and made me suffer. He gave me purpose! All those years I toiled away in misery as a lowly corporate slave to support my family when I could have been so much more; when I should have been so much more... All those years wasted working long hours day and night doing what I was told. I barely saw my babies grow up to be children before they were killed." Merrill lamented.

Merrill then added, "I was always more than just an insignificant average nobody! You should have found me as a child like you found your Ninja Mice. You should have trained me to become extraordinary like you're training your darling ninjas. All those years I suffered neeclessly because no one recognized my gifts. I could have saved my family had someone taught me how to use my powers earlier or. My family would still be alive today!"

"Thou anger has given thee great power. But if thou alloweth, the anger shall undo thee. What thou seeketh is not justice; tis vengeance. Justice is about harmony and restoring balance and order. Avenging the death of thy family shall not bring them back. It shall not make thee whole. Thou seeketh vengeance to make thyself feel better. But an eye for an eye shall certainly make the world blind. Goldmouse hath made thou a monster." said Greenspan.

"I have made him a force to be reckoned with; a powerful Asumari warrior to be feared. You call him a monster. I call him my greatest creation." said Goldmouse as he and Madolf picked themselves up from the beating they received earlier to join Merrill Pynch in surrounding Greenspan.

"The rage that drives thee is an immeasurable anger that hath consumed thy grief. For to fill the void left by the loss, thou hath replace grief with hate. Memory of your loved ones is now just poison in your veins. Someday you may find yourself wishing the family you loved had never existed, so you'd be spared your pain. But there is still good in thee." said Greenspan to Merrill. "Thou doth not have to continue down this dark path. Let go of the hate. Let go of the poison that runs through your vein."

Pausing for a moment, Merrill reluctantly says, "It's too late for me. I have embraced my dark side and have committed too many unspeakable acts of evil. In the name of vengeance, I have acted out of anger and hate. Too much blood has been spilt and I have lashed out and hurt too many innocent beings to be forgiven. I cannot turn back now.'

"By 3 methods we may learn wisdom: First, by reflection, which is noblest. Second, by imitation, which is easiest. And third by experience, which is the bitterest." Greenspan explained quoting **Confucius**. "The reason it is too late for thee is because thou believeth true. Though nobody can go back and make a new beginning, anyone can start over and make a new ending. Every passing minute, every passing day, is another chance to turn it all around. So it is never too late to be what thou might have been."

> **Thou art not born a dark tyrant being**
> **Thou art born a slate; to choose and create**
> **Thou art monster made; from anger and hate**
> **Choose the light and kindness you've stopped seeing**
> **Choose to be good for it is not too late**
>
> **Thou art the sum of the choices thou made**
> **In time and circumstances fair or nay**
> **On divergent paths that seem equal lay**
> **Evil results from bad choices unswayed**
> **But past is not fate when we turn away**

"He has made his choice. We all have!" Goldmouse proclaimed as he, Madolf and Merrill all close in on Greenspan. "We have chosen to be great and powerful. We have chosen to be rulers of the world rather than to be ruled. You, on the other hand, have chosen to be a servant to the weak and stand in our way."

Greenspan is surrounded by his enemies with nowhere to go. They close in on him. But Greenspan is unafraid. He truly believes there is still good in Merrill and hopes that he will turn away from his dark side. "If it is me fate to die this day, then so be it. But what I stand for and what I teach will not. I shall not fight thee." said Greenspan to Merrill as he drops his defensive posture.

Greenspan's earlier words weigh heavily on Merrill as he sees the old mouse completely fearless in the face of certain death. He begins to feel remorse and regret for the blood thirsty monster he had become. Merrill is conflicted as he senses there is truth to what Greenspan had said.

> I am now old and grey and full of sleep
> Strike me down you may; defeat I am not
> Thou art a pawn in someone else's plot
> Follow orders if thou must, like a sheep.
> With my passing my powers I shall keep
>
> What shall ye accomplish by killing thee?
> Your remaining days shall be filled with dread
> By shadows that seek to avenge my death
> Seek instead a path that won't take your breath
> A path with least suffering and bloodshed

After speaking, Greenspan puts himself into a deep hibernation state. His breathing and heartbeat stops almost completely as cocoons himself into a ball. Goldmouse can't believe his eyes or ears as he is now faced with an unexpected choice.

"Shall I destroy him now, Master?" Merrill asked Goldmouse.

"No, we can use him for leverage and ransom." Goldmouse replied. "Greenspan is correct. If we kill him, the Ninja Mice will surely seek to avenge his death just as you seek to avenge the death of your family. We can instead, use Greenspan to lure the mice into a trap. Our gold is buried under the collapsed factory. We can make the Ninja Mice retrieve our gold for us and trade Greenspan for the Gold. When they show up for the trade, we can kill them all at once. And if we do it on a full moon, we may even take Greenspan's powers!"

"That's genius!" Madolf praised Goldmouse.

Together, the intruders all leave with Greenspan's body in their custody. They also leave a ransom note for the Ninja Mice to find. By the time the mice arrive home from the candy store, they are too late. They find a chaotic scene of destruction and damage. The mice observe there obviously was a struggle earlier at the dojo. They find no sign of their Grandmaster but Knyse does find the ransom note left for them. Together the mice read the note and are horrified.

If you ever want to see your Grandmaster alive again, retrieve the buried gold at the factory and bring it to me and I will trade your Grandmaster for my gold.

TO BE CONTINUED...